For my Zandria

*For the women in my life
who have shown me
the best of what Motherhood should be*

What others are saying about Mark Miller's writing...

"...a well-crafted piece of literature with many unexpected twists and turns throughout..."

-Amazon Review

"Miller has a lot of whatever it is that makes a good fantasy writer...Whatever the secret is to writing great fantasy, The Secret Queen is the result."

-Reader's Favorite Book Reviews

"There is a musical quality to the way Miller writes that makes the reader want to pick up more of his books. Something else that should be considered is that these books have very strong female protagonists, none of the wimpy ones we see too often nowadays, so it's a great choice for teen girls."

-Midwest Book Reviews

"From trials and victories, battles and moments of heartwarming scenarios, The Fourth Queen is a novel the entire family will find enjoyable... His vivid and descriptive narratives portray him as a master of the craft."

-Amazon Review

Books by Mark Miller

The Empyrical Tales
Book I: Journey of the Fourth Queen
Book II: Search for the Lost Queen
Book III: Mystery of the Secret Queen
Book IV: History of the First Queen

Small World Global Protection Agency
#001 New Kids on the Rock
#002 Bulls and Burglars
#003 The Not So Perfect Game

Promise of Tomorrow

THE EMPYRICAL TALES BOOK II

SEARCH FOR THE LOST QUEEN

Mark Miller

MillerWords, LLC

MillerWords, LLC
PO Box 861074
Shawnee, KS 66286

First Edition

For discounts on bulk purchases, please contact MillerWords Educational Sales at **Sales@MillerWords.com**

Printed in the United States of America

2 4 6 8 10 9 7 5 3 1

Library of Congress Control Number: 2018900432

ISBN: 978-0-9996195-2-0

Chapter 1

It All Starts With a Bang

Zandria loved the feel of the warm, wet sand squishing between her toes. It meant that she was safe. This was important to her because she had not felt safe for a long time. Here on the beach of Banookanook, she was protected. To the north and south stood the rock walls that cut their village off from the rest of the world. Behind her grew a nearly impassable jungle and in front of her lie the unending sea.

She wriggled her toes against the mounting sand and decided it was time to rinse her feet in the clear water. Zandria waded out to her knees and let the rhythmic waves clean her toes and feet. She was on the beach with no greater purpose than playing with her sister, Olena.

They were four years apart in age and sometimes that made all the difference in the world. Yet, sometimes, they were as close as if they shared one mind and one heart. Today was one of those days. There were no sisterly quarrels, only laughing. Neither could do anything to upset the other. Zandria did not even scream when Olena snuck up behind and splashed her.

The cold water on her head and shoulders shocked goose pimples across her skin. She turned to her curly haired sister in time to see the smaller girl knocked flat by an unexpected wave. This erupted more laughter from both of them.

The sound must have been louder than Zandria realized because it caught the attention of her father. He walked out of their small hut with her mother following close behind. They were holding hands and smiling.

This made Zandria's heart feel like it was going to burst with love. She waited for six years to see her mother again. Around the time of Olena's birth was when she saw her last. She was angry with herself for forgetting how beautiful the woman was. There was no doubt in Zandria's mind that this woman should be one of the four queens of Empyrean. Zandria saw that she stood slightly taller than her father and carried her slender body with grace. Looking at her mother now, she could see more of Olena in her.

She did not want to turn away from this chance to hug her mother and hold onto her, but the ocean spray kept getting in her face. Zandria tried to wipe the water away, still it clouded her eyes and blurred her vision. The more she brushed her face with the backs of her fists, the more water flooded her eyes. Suddenly, the bright sun faded to darkness and she was alone.

Zandria woke in her bed at the Castle Empyrean surrounded by darkness with tears in her eyes. She instantly realized she was dreaming about her mother. The spray from the ocean was actually her own crying. The thought of that imaginary day on the beach that could never happen tore at her emotions with both love and hate. The anger disappeared quickly because she was not that person anymore. Instead, she chose to remember her with the love and kindness that she knew her mother would have.

She laid in her bed, staring at the ceiling with drying tears on her cheeks. The battle was over and the celebration feast earlier that evening was amazing. Zandria still felt stuffed because she ate like she had not eaten in a month. The stress and fear of her journey from Banookanook to the castle took its toll on her, but finally she was able to rest and recover. The Forgotten Evil was defeated, at least for now, and she could be at peace knowing that Olena was the fourth queen.

That is when she heard it, a faint sound of crying.

At first, Zandria thought it was her imagination. So many memories flashed through her head. She thought the crying might be an echo of her dream. Then she considered it might be her sister trying to cope with the recent events. As she lay there, she thought of the werewolves, the animals of Bremen, Baba Yaga and the bottomless canyon beneath the bell chamber. Even the thought of the entire castle hanging out over that same nothingness would be enough to bother her.

Through all her mind's wandering, in the dark of her bedroom, the distant crying did not stop. Zandria felt it to be a very lonely sobbing. After their victory on the battlefield and Olena becoming queen, how could anybody in Empyrean be sad, especially her sister?

Zandria decided to ignore the sound, since she believed it was only in her imagination. She tried to sleep and buried herself in the overly fluffy covers. She drifted off for an instant, but snapped wide-awake and her whole body jolted like she was falling out of bed. She was not falling, though the sensation made her think of the canyon again. Zandria did not like when she woke for no reason.

The room was not any lighter since the last time she opened her eyes. It was still the middle of the night. Like most of the rooms in the castle, her room had no windows. Somehow, moonlight magically refracted or reflected its way inside and she could make out the glistening outlines of her crystal bedposts and the tall, glass dresser by the wall. Still, the opulent room did not feel quite like home.

She was not scared to be sleeping alone. After all, she was in the safest place in all of Empyrean. She knew Olena or the other queens would come if she called, along with a hundred other attendants or soldiers. Plus, her friend Adam's room was close.

Zandria liked the thought of him being near. He proved himself to her while getting her across the plains and into the castle. When she first met him, she did not trust him, but that feeling was always outmatched by those pestering butterflies in her stomach. She knew it would take a long time to get used to those butterflies, if ever, she thought. That was okay for now, she decided.

Now, she listened again for the crying sound, thinking she would not hear it. Whatever trick her mind was playing on her, the crying was still there.

She knew there was nothing else to do now, except find this exceptionally sad person. Zandria swung her legs out of bed. Her bare feet only touched the cold glass floor for a moment, before recoiling back. She found her slippers tucked slightly back behind the dust ruffle. She tried them on and, despite all of the magic surrounding her, found them to be completely uncomfortable and not at all her size.

Zandria left her room barefoot. She followed the crying sound as it gradually became louder. Still not convinced that it was real, she continued searching. Enthralled by the sound, she moved through the castle not attempting to keep track of her many turns and the transforming hallways behind her. Apparently, no one else could hear the crying as she did not bump into anyone else along the way. This fact also made her believe she imagined the sound.

At last, she came to a wooden door that was strangely out of place in its crystal surroundings. The door was made from an oily, black wood. This sight alone made her not want to open it. Zandria was certain the sound, now clearly crying, was coming from the other side. She was no longer certain it was only in her imagination. She did not go in right away, instead listening to the tears and gentle sobs. The sound seemed so close, almost in her head, yet so far away at the same time.

Carefully putting her hand on the glass knob, chills ran up her spine. The knob was not cold, as she expected, but Zandria instantly got the feeling that she did not want to know what was on the other side.

Maybe the old Zandria would have walked away, she thought, but not this new version. This Zandria felt the true power of Empyrean still warm in her heart and was literally an arm's reach away from being the fourth queen. She would never again let fear stop her. She knew that as long as she believed with her heart, everything would turn out right. Whatever waited on the other side of this door, she thought, could not hurt her or possibly even affect her in any way.

She turned the knob and opened the door.

The room was not much different than any of the others she had seen in Empyrean. The floor and ceiling were made of glass, but the walls were very narrow like she was walking into a hallway, or more likely, a closet. At the far end of the room stood a short pillar and on top of the pillar lay a small white pillow. The pillow looked as smooth as silk and had white tassels dangling from each of its four corners.

Nestled in the center of the pillow was a single crystal shard. Now, Zandria knew the crying was coming from that crystal. She smiled to herself, thinking how silly it would be for a piece of glass to be crying. Then she realized the sound was not coming from the crystal itself, but rather from inside it. That is why it still sounded so far away even though she was right next to it.

Zandria looked down at the shard. It was narrow and would easily fit in her hand like an oversized hairbrush handle. The inside of the crystal looked smoky, but it cleared as she gazed closer.

Then, through the mist, she saw a woman holding her head in her hands. Zandria knew this was the person that kept her from sleeping. She could hear this woman's haunting cry across the entire castle. She suspected the sad woman could not see outside of the crystal even if her long, wavy brown hair was not hanging in her face.

Suddenly, the woman turned and looked straight out at Zandria. She stopped crying in a single breath, looking fierce and frightened at the same time. For an instant, Zandria thought she was looking at Olena as a grown woman. Then she realized who it was.

Zandria said, "Mother?"

Her mother looked directly at her and said, "Zandria. Please help me."

The crystal swirled with smoke again and the face disappeared. Zandria turned to get help. Not knowing, of its own accord, the door swung closed behind her, she ran face-first into the thick wood.

BANG.

Everything went black.

Zandria awoke in her bed. The brightness of the room told her it was morning. She immediately thought of her mother trapped in that crystal.

Then she wondered how she got back to her room. The throbbing in her head told her it was not a dream and a study of her reflection in the mirror confirmed it with a bruise on her right cheek. Something was not right about the whole experience, she thought.

Forgetting the mystery of returning to bed, she quickly threw on one of the thirty dresses she was given. Zandria ran to her bedroom door and flung it open to find Tym, the elf, waiting for her.

"Good morning, my dear. Are you ready for breakfast?" he said.

Zandria was glad he was there. Tym was one of the castle's caretakers and knew many secrets of navigating the ever-changing passages because he was born within its walls. He could quickly take her to Olena. She started out the door, not noticing that Tym already had another companion.

Adam said, "Hi." Then after an inward gasp of air, "That's a nasty bruise. It must be left over from the shipwreck."

"No, I didn't get it on The Dragon's Wing. It happened last night," she said.

"Bump into a wall trying to find your way to the bathroom?" Adam said with a laugh.

Adam's sense of humor brought a smile to Zandria's face, but she had more pressing concerns. "I'll explain it all, but I need to see Olena now," she said. As an afterthought, she added, "And the other queens."

Tym must have read the seriousness of her face and led the way without another word. As they twisted and turned their way along, Adam continually examined her face. Zandria felt herself becoming slightly annoyed, but at the same time, she enjoyed the attention.

Soon, they were in the dining hall where the four queens were finishing an exuberant breakfast with their assorted guests. Zandria rushed to Olena.

"I saw her," she said.

Olena, the Queen of the Eastern Sky, looked confused and a little startled by Zandria's behavior. "Who did you see, Zan?" she said, picking over the last of some enormous blue grapes.

"Our mother. She's alive."

"Dear," interrupted Snow White, the Queen of the Northern Wood. "Your mother was lost six years ago. You know that."

Isis, the Queen of the Southern Valley, added, "I'm afraid that bump on your head has given you some bad dreams."

"I know. I know all that," said Zandria. "I know where she was lost. I saw her trapped in a crystal last night. I can show it to you if I can find the room again."

Cinderella, the Queen of the Western Sun, said, "If that is the case, we must get to her at once. Which room is it?"

"All I remember is that it had a black wooden door. That's how I got this," Zandria said, pointing at her injured cheek.

"That is impossible. There is no Blackwood within these walls," said Tym.

"I do not mean to belittle what you saw," said Snow White, "but I believe it was simply a hallucination."

"It is true that bumps to the head have caused many people to see and hear strange things," said Cinderella.

Frustrated that they were dismissing it so easily, Zandria said, "But I saw her. We have to help her."

Isis said, "It was a bad dream, dear. That is all. Now sit and eat. You will feel better."

"You believe me, don't you?" Zandria asked Olena.

"Sure, but..." Olena looked to the other queens. None of them made eye contact, leaving Zandria to wonder what was not being said.

At that, Prince William stood up from his mostly finished plate of eggs. "If you'll excuse me, Miss Zandria. I do not want to interrupt such important matters, but now that young Adam is awake, I must discuss our impending journey with him."

Distracted from the thoughts of her mother, Zandria turned to Adam. "What journey? Where are you going?"

Adam looked apologetic. "We decided last night that we should head back to the Rockhorn mines as soon as possible. If there are any other slaves there, we should rescue them."

"I can help you find the children," Zandria said. If no one wanted to help her find her mother, she wanted to be doing something. She especially did not want to be left alone right now.

"Considering your present condition, it may be better for you to stay here," said William.

"I can't sit around doing nothing," Zandria said.

Adam took her hand and moved to a corner away from the breakfast crowd. He said, "For what it's worth, I believe you saw *something* last night. I don't know if it was your mother, but I'm willing to believe anything is possible here. These mines could be dangerous, especially if any of the dwarves or Rockhorns are still there. Stay here and maybe you will find your missing room. At least I know you will be safe."

"And why do you care that I'm safe?" Zandria said faking irritation.

"Because I care. That's all."

Adam glanced to see William waiting with another elf by the door. He gently squeezed Zandria's hand and left the room.

As if it was not bad enough that no one believed her about her mother, she was now doubly embarrassed in front of the four queens. She plopped down in her seat and silently began eating her quickly cooling porridge.

Chapter 2

Down, Down, Down

Fury stood at the head of the bridge waiting for the travelers to depart. Adam looked at the strong, black horse and could see why William was disappointed not to be riding him. Most of the Friesians and their men were returning to the Northern Wood, but Fury was staying at the castle with Snow White.

"I wish I was going with you," said Fury to William.

"Your place is here now, my friend," said William. "Besides, the steeds you recommended will be fine traveling companions."

Adam watched the men saddle the two horses that Fury chose to take them back east. Fury explained they were his old stablemates and the last to complete their training under Wrath, Fury's predecessor. Adam did not know Fury as well as William did, but both the man and horse helped

Zandria make it to the castle so he knew he could trust them.

"Kalis and Sulis are the only two in the north to ever beat me in a race and only once," Fury said. "Don't say anything to them or you'll never hear the end of it. They'll suit you well, especially coming from Wrath's stock."

"You mean *student*?" Adam thought Fury used the wrong word.

"That too," said Fury. "It's never been confirmed, but the rumor is Wrath is their father. I always said the old nag had a way with the mares." Adam did not know horses could have facial expressions, but to him, Fury looked coy right now.

"Speaking of, where is your former boss?" asked William. "I would like to bid him farewell." Adam watched William scan the crowded courtyard.

"Me too," said Adam. What little he knew of the Friesians, he actually knew Wrath better and genuinely wanted to say goodbye. He never had the chance to thank Wrath for carrying him and Zandria to the secret entrance which led them into the castle.

"The unicorns left at sunrise and Wrath decided to go with Sayonya. They said they were heading east. If they can find a way to cross the Great Cliffs, there are supposed to be endless pastures to the far south."

William looked lost in memory for a moment. Adam guessed the five hundred year old man had once seen those pastures.

"I can tell you first hand, the cliffs are far easier going down," said Adam, wanting to be part of the conversation. He remembered his jump from the waterfall when he first started chasing Zandria.

One of the western stablehands walked with Kalis and Sulis. He bowed in front of William when he presented the reins to them.

"That is not necessary. Please stand up, boy," said William.

"Sorry sir. Being that you are a prince, it's forced by habit," said the boy. "We are very formal where I come from." Adam thought this stablehand looked somewhere in age between William and himself. He felt bad that so many innocent young people were forced into the recent war.

"There is nothing wrong with manners, but I'm a person same as you." William patted the blue-uniformed boy on the shoulder. Then he mounted Sulis like an agile youth. William looked down at the boy and asked, "What is your name?"

"Humboldt, sir," said the stablehand, appearing quite shy.

"Well, mount up Hum. Unless you don't plan to sleep at the foot of the Euphoric Mountains tomorrow night," said William. Adam felt the contagiousness of William's excitement. He quickly looked to his own Friesian.

Humboldt ran back to his horse and Adam climbed atop Kalis. Adam glanced back across the courtyard at their party of fifty or so. Men, women and animals from the North, South, East and West volunteered to help rescue the slave children. It amazed Adam how other people could be so giving and caring. This was something he never experienced underground. The rest of the crowd were making their own preparations for returning to their various homes. Adam wondered what it would feel like to have a home. Then he thought of the mines and sadly realized that was where he was going.

William whistled and waved his hand. The line of horses and carts moved across the temporary bridge made from the wreckage of the Dragon's Wing and a few other ships destroyed in the battle. A giant golden crocodile followed behind with its stunning mistress standing proudly on its back.

Fury yelled to them, "Safe journey and may Evorin's breath be at your back."

William leaned toward Adam and with a boyish grin said, "Not too close I hope. Yeeouch." He pantomimed having his backside burned.

Adam looked at the man and smiled at the joke. His momentary homesickness faded. There was something familiar about this longhaired prince. He knew William came from the Dead Forest, or as he called it, the Royal Forest. Adam also knew he was over five hundred years old. Still, he felt a kinship with him. No less than a dozen people remarked as to how much they looked alike at the feast last night. Adam never had a family and this made him wonder what became of William's family. He also knew the prince was trapped in ice and never married. Thinking the man could never have had any children, Adam pushed the thought out of his head. In a way, he felt they were both alone.

Their journey across the plains passed uneventful. A few fires still burned the tall grass, but they saw the occasional crews of different pirate ships working diligently to put out the flames. Prince William's Parade, as Adam thought of it, maintained a comfortable pace and as William predicted, they camped in the foothills of the Euphoric Mountains on the second night.

William recounted the plan again before they went to sleep. Adam understood that they would travel the Great Road as far east as the Palace by the Sea if there was need. As they crossed the wasteland, if the scouts could find a way down, they would enter the mines there. Otherwise, it was suggested the best place to start looking was the hole in the ground that marked Adam's return to Empyrean.

This hole signified Adam's escape. It was also the only place he had ever lived. He desperately wanted a real home, but knew that would not happen without the closure of his time as a slave.

Lying at the base of the enormous purple and gray mountains, Adam tried to brighten his mood and almost looked forward to their task. Being this close to the mountains, their entire party was feeling the magical effects of euphoria. Everyone slept peacefully and woke in splendid moods. Adam was delighted to learn that the Great Road passed straight through the mountains without having to do any climbing.

He kept thinking ahead to their stop in Bremen. He wondered if Lady Mulgart and her baby would still be there.

The possibility of seeing her again left him with a strange longing. He remembered her being a caring mother and wondered if there was a possibility of having a home with the two of them.

In another two days' time, the parade arrived in the animal town of Bremen. Mayor Virgata, the white tiger, greeted them like royalty. Adam was surprised by the amount of repair that had already been done. There was no sign of the explosion that destroyed the poison rock or any fighting that littered the roads the last time he was there. Instead of the straw huts, the assorted animals now made homes in the buildings left by the people and opened two of the inns as proper businesses.

Adam found the brown ox that once traveled with Lady Mulgart and eagerly asked about her and the baby.

"I don't know where she went," said the ox in a slow, sad voice. Adam found himself to be somewhat sad about it as well. He wanted to see her mostly because of the thoughts that were ricocheting in his head these past several days. First it was Zandria and her sister, then the queens, then everyone telling him he looked like William. For the first time in his life, he knew what it felt like to have a family and yet still be so alone. He knew she already had a baby and he did not know her at all, but Adam toyed with the idea of calling Lady Mulgart his mother. Since she was not here, none of that mattered now.

Before leaving the next morning, Virgata offered the assistance of several moles to help navigate the dark passages. Adam watched William graciously accept and the small creatures were put under the care of Humboldt, or Hum as William insisted on calling him. Adam shared the excitement of the parade leaving Bremen as if it were a real celebration. All of the animals came out and lined the roads to watch them go. They were wished farewell and cheered on by a melodious variety of brays, barks and chirps.

Adam spent a lot of his traveling in silence. Kalis and Sulis did not even have half as much to say as Fury and William stayed busy with the scouts. The Prince continued sending them off the Great Road as they crossed the wasteland. To Adam's disappointment, the reports did not vary much. The scouts could not find a way down into the Rockhorn mines.

This quiet gave Adam time to think. First, he thought about Lady Mulgart. He realized his feelings had nothing to do with her. He simply wanted a mother, or some family that he could call his own. His whole life, he was alone, but he was never aware of the feeling until he saw how wonderful it could be not to be alone.

Maybe, he wondered, that is why he felt such a connection with Zandria. She lost both her parents and, from a certain perspective, her sister too. He knew her situation was not the same, but, at least, he felt something in common with her. Adam wished she was here now. Then he double-wished that she was not because he knew what dangers might await them when they go down.

The second thing he thought about was that they were getting closer to that dreadful hole in the ground. They had to go through Edge Town next to the Palace by the Sea to get there. He could not remember doing anything particularly bad, but was afraid the people there might remember him. Before coming above ground, he never cared what others thought of him or his actions. Now having someone to care for, he felt this was a good change. Also, he was beginning to feel like he did not want to go back into those caves.

The last thing Adam contemplated on their trip was William. Despite being frozen, the prince did not really look that much older than he did. He seemed older when he met him the day of the battle, but Adam spent more time with him lately. Now, his old urges kicked in and he did not want to be outdone by someone like William. He believed he could be as brave and as tough as William. It was his responsibility to lead them into the hole in the ground at the Palace by the Sea. He could not let himself be afraid. He was going to be the first to go down.

In only a few days, they crossed the entire wasteland, entered the jungle and now stood at the center of Edge Town, the small market-village at the gates of the Palace by the Sea. Somewhat to Adam's relief, the town appeared deserted. They soon found out that the palace was abandoned as well.

With the passing of the previous Queen of the Eastern Sky, the palace was already beginning to crumble. The magic that held the smooth, spiraling columns of sand started to fade with that woman. Adam guessed that Queen Olena would have plenty of rebuilding to do when it was time to move back to the palace. Then he saw William looking as if someone had punched him in the stomach.

Adam slid down from Kalis and joined the prince on the ground. Up close, he could see the young man had tears in his eyes as well. "What is it?"

"This place is miraculous," said William.

"It is beautiful," answered Adam. With the way it was already starting to fall apart, he guessed the beauty would not last long, especially if a storm came up over the sea.

"I knew her, you know. I can see her in this place. Only she could have created something like this," said William. Then he sucked in a breath, wiped his face with his sleeve and said, "Time to get to work." Adam secretly envied the man's apparent ability to control his emotions. He did not think he could do the same, but he would try.

With the size of the hole in the courtyard, the horses and crocodile remained in the market of Edge Town. A few carts were brought inside the palace gate and the men unloaded their contents. After an hour's work, they had constructed several pulleys and lifts on the side of the chasm. With the help of the Friesians, these platforms would lower them into the ground much faster than climbing the jagged walls down.

Adam made it a point to be in the first search party. He felt a mix of guilty responsibility and competitiveness. He was joined by Hum and his moles along with two dark skinned Southerners. They were lowered slowly into the darkness. As they went down, Adam's eyes became accustomed to the lack of light. For too many years, these stony walls were the only thing he saw. For him, the smell was worse. Before, it was something he was used to, but now he realized what it was. The rotting smell of countless slaves used and discarded over one hundred years poisoned the air.

This knowledge caused Adam to get sick and he lost his breakfast over the rail of their basket. It only took a moment for the wet mess to slosh against the rock floor and he knew they were at the bottom. With the people clear of the platform, the horses immediately pulled it up, but Adam could already make out another basket being lowered next to it.

Hum bent low to the ground and let his two moles loose. They scurried off into the black intent on finding any surviving children. Adam needed a moment to recover and took it when he saw William in the second basket. While he waited, Adam examined the very chamber where the evil mutated snail General Gusk set him to his original task of stopping a young girl from becoming queen. Adam regained some strength in knowing that he was instrumental in stopping their wicked plans.

Finally, William organized the rescue and the search started. The whole thing moved surprisingly fast as Adam led them through painfully familiar halls to the main chamber where most of the children were waiting. He found them to be too scared to try to escape. None of them admitted knowing there was a way out or if they should try it before the dwarves came back with their stone monsters. One of the older girls spoke for the weary group.

She said, "One of the dwarves stayed here with us. When he heard you coming, he went back there." She pointed at a tunnel that Adam remembered too well. Not knowing it was forbidden, he once tried to go down that tunnel looking for food. He was beaten as punishment and could not walk for three days. He knew even a lone dwarf was enough to keep these tortured children from escaping.

Adam explained to William, "Whatever's through there, the dwarves never wanted anyone to see it."

"Then that's where we must go," said William.

Reluctantly, with the scars on his back reminding him of his fear, Adam followed. They left the others behind to start leading the children above ground. The tunnel was considerably narrower and less designed for humans than dwarves and children. In several spaces, Adam had to turn sideways and duck his head to make it through. He could not imagine how William fit behind him.

They eventually emerged in a small room, lit by a torch mounted crudely to the wall. This room had two passages leading further underground.

"Pick one," William said.

Adam walked into the left passage without a word. At this point, he was not trying to be braver than William. In fact, he was too scared to make a sound. He looked behind him to see William enter the other passage and then he was alone, again. Adam moved on in the dark, holding his breath and letting his fingers guide him along the wall. His breath tightened in his chest. Before long, he was crawling to keep moving forward and his head bumped against a solid surface. Even his eyes could not see what it was, but his hands felt greasy wood instead of rock. This was some kind of door.

He pushed hard and the door popped open. The well-lit room temporarily blinded Adam. It took him a moment to focus and then he clearly saw the room full of treasure. Mostly it was swamped in gold coins, rings and trinkets all reflecting the light of the ornate candle chandelier overhead. Aside from gold, there were too many other prizes for Adam to remember, but he imagined what Zandria would say if he brought her back a few necklaces and rings.

Then something unusual caught his eye. On one of the piles lay a slender, pointed crystal. It did not look like a piece of jewelry, but he thought it was about the size and shape of a dagger. He thought it especially strange that the crystal seemed to be filled with smoke. Adam picked it up to examine it more closely and then heard a noise behind him. He turned around in time to see the slimy black door slam shut as the sneaking dwarf slipped past him.

"William! He's getting away!" shouted Adam. He pulled hard in a panic and yanked the small door off its hinges. He did not want to return to this place only for it to become his tomb. Adam crawled as fast as he could back up the tunnel, the rocky surface making small cuts on his hands and knees. Finally, he rolled out into the antechamber and landed next to the dwarf.

The dwarf still had William's sword in him and Adam looked up to see William standing over them. Adam did not know whether to scream or laugh. He wanted to scream and be out of these mines forever. However, seeing William's pants around his ankles made him want to laugh. William was holding his belt, not paying attention to Adam or the dispatched dwarf.

"What are you doing?" asked Adam.

William looked as equally confused. He said, "I drew my sword and I'm not sure what happened. My belt must have come unhitched, but I didn't want the cretin to escape. Pride goes before the pants and all that."

Adam waited, staring at the body of the dwarf, while William adjusted his pants.

"I want to show you what's down here," said William, gesturing to his passage. "First, what is it that you've found?"

Adam did not realize that he stuck the crystal into his waistband before escaping the treasure chamber. He held it up in the torch light to see that the inside still looked smoky.

"Zandria was talking about crystals before we left, so I thought I would bring this back to her." He improvised his explanation to hide his panicked reaction. Somehow, he felt the crystal was more important than the gold and decided to leave the treasure buried.

William led Adam down the other passage, not nearly as narrow, into a room filled with shelves of scrolls. One scroll was rolled out on a table in the center of the room.

"It appears that our thieving friends were fond of keeping records. I suspect these pages tell the names and towns of every child they kidnapped over the years. This one is of particular interest," said William. He pointed at the scroll on the table and Adam leaned over, unable to make out the chaotic lines.

"I can't read," he said without embarrassment.

"Forgive me," said William. "It states 'Boy, Adam, Town, Bond'."

"Is that where I'm from?" Adam asked excitedly.

William struggled with his belt again, "My apologies, I really don't know what is the problem with my wardrobe. But yes, it appears a boy named Adam was taken from the town of Bond eleven years ago today."

Adam's mind raced. Somewhere, there could be a family waiting for him. "Where's Bond?"

"Somewhere in the Royal Forest, I am sure. Alas, it did not exist in my time. The Palace above our heads may hold that answer. One thing is certain though."

"What's that?" asked Adam.

"Today we celebrate your birthday," said William.

By the time Adam and William made it back through the main hall, they learned that the last of the children were found. William suggested he and Adam exit the caves last. Adam truly wanted to be above ground, but agreed the other children needed to be freed first.

While they waited for their basket to take them to the surface, Adam examined the crystal again. As he watched, the smoke cleared and a brown haired woman appeared. Adam swore she looked exactly like Zandria, but William later insisted she more closely resembled Olena.

The woman spoke, "Follow the crystal, Adam. You must help me." Then she was gone and the smoky swirling returned.

Adam looked to see if William heard her. His look of astonishment proved he did.

"What should I do?" asked Adam.

"She called you by name, my boy. What choice do you have? Let's get to the surface and form a plan."

Adam climbed onto the waiting platform, followed by William tugging at his oddly loose pants.

Chapter 3

The Sight Unseen

She never imagined it could happen in this fantastic castle, but Zandria felt bored. Adam had only been gone for a day, but it seemed like one of the longest days of her life. The queens kept Olena in private chambers for her training and most of the volunteer soldiers were returning to their distant homes. Zandria desperately needed some company or something to do.

After the incident that resulted in her bruised cheek, Zandria was instructed not to roam the castle alone. The queens were overly nice, but being sent to her room felt like punishment. Because of that, the only time she was allowed to leave her room was when Tym came to take her to the banquet hall for meals. Zandria told herself she could not simply sit in her room playing with dolls like a little kid. After all, she was almost eleven.

The morning that Adam and William crossed the Euphoric Mountains with their rescue party, Zandria was determined to do something different. At least, she wanted some new company. Kez remained constantly with Olena and Zandria had no one else. So after breakfast, she asked Tym to take her to the stables. After glancing to the other queens for approval, he agreed.

Zandria found Fury, looking groomed and quite handsome, in the center of several beautiful golden Andalusian mares telling them a story. She missed the first part of his tale, but she knew what happened because she was there.

"Then the dragon blocked the passage with his tail, cutting us off from the queen and her sister," said Fury. Zandria did not feel uncomfortable because the stable was very clean. She started to make a seat on some fresh straw.

She saw the mares looking enthralled and impressed with the brave Friesian. However, Fury's choice of words slightly hurt her feelings. He did not even use her name and instead called her the *sister*. For Zandria's entire life, it was always *Zandria and Olena*. In everything they did, Zandria was always named first. While she could not be happier for Olena, it was a strange feeling to seem suddenly less important.

"Good morning," said Fury. He trotted towards Zandria saying, "Ladies, this is the brave young girl I was telling you about."

Zandria liked how Fury interrupted his story to come say hello to her. Then she felt the warmth in her heart that was planted there in the bell chamber. She truly knew she was not less important than Olena. She realized that her worth had nothing to do with her title and everything to do with the friends that cared for her. The loneliness of the past few days must be getting to her, she thought.

She said, "I'm sorry, General. I didn't mean to interrupt your story. Please continue."

"This is an excellent stopping point. It'll keep everyone in suspense as to how we escaped from the dragon. I would much rather visit with you. It feels like I haven't seen you in days," said Fury.

"And I would much rather hear about Evorin," said Zandria. "William wouldn't tell either." She really wanted to know what happened after her and Olena ran down the mountain. She thought Fury and William were going to be eaten by Evorin. She was so happy to see them alive after the Rockhorn battle, but did not know how they made it out of the Euphoric Mountains.

Fury lowered his head, "I must confess. The dragon made us swear never to tell you or your sister. Besides, you know how the story ends and that's what's important."

"What could be the big secret?" asked Zandria, growing a little impatient.

"Trust me, it's not that interesting. If you don't mind, I'd like to talk about something else before I start to look like a liar in front of the mares over there," said Fury.

Zandria could tell he was sincere and decided to leave it alone. She knew someone would tell her the story eventually. Besides, there was something else she wanted to talk about, her mother. The elder queens either did not believe her or did not want to believe her. Maybe, she hoped, Fury would have some answers.

"I think I found my mother," she said.

"I didn't know she was lost," replied Fury.

"You mean you don't know who my mother is?" Zandria was surprised by this. She thought someone in his position should know. Then she wondered if her mother's disappearance was important to anyone other than her.

"I'm afraid I don't, but I suspect you're about to tell me," Fury answered.

"She disappeared right after Olena was born," explained Zandria. "The Queen of the Eastern Sky said my mother was going to be the next queen and sent her off for training. She left the Palace by the Sea and no one has seen her since."

"You mean your mother is the Lost Queen?" exclaimed Fury.

Now Zandria wondered if the woman was more important than she guessed. While it saddened her, she was also impressed that her mother at least had a title. "She never got to be queen though."

"True, but that's what she is called out of respect," said Fury. "This story is doubly amazing. First that Olena is so young and now that the line is passed through birth. The crown has never stayed with the same blood before."

"My father said it was supposed to. That's why he sent us," she said. She did not think it unusual that a mother and daughter could both be in line to be queen.

"I'm no expert," said Fury, "but knowing which family the queen comes from would make things pretty dangerous for their descendants, I fear."

She could attest to the danger, but knew the power of Empyrean was stronger. She hoped that power could protect potential queens.

"But you said she is known here," pleaded Zandria.

"I know she's been talked about, but that was a few years ago. The subject is avoided because of a curse, I think. The only other thing I know is that the story has to do with a crystal," said Fury.

Zandria became uncontrollably excited, "I saw the crystal."

"Which crystal?" asked Fury.

"The one my mother's trapped in. I found a room the other night and the crystal was there."

"I don't know about that, but the topic of the crystal is not spoken about either. I'm sorry that I can't do more. If the queens won't speak of it, I don't think you'll get much help from anyone else," said Fury.

"That's okay. I can't find the room anymore either," said Zandria dejectedly.

"Maybe that's what you should concentrate on," said Fury.

Zandria hugged the horse around his neck and left the stable thinking about how to find the crystal again. She was a little disappointed that he could not help. Still, she now had more information than when she started. Tym met her at the top of the steps across the courtyard and led her back to her room. That night, she lay awake, straining her ears for the crying that would lead her back to the hidden room. She hoped the Lost Queen would call for her again.

No sound came.

On the same morning that Adam's rescue party made it to the Palace by the Sea, Zandria had breakfast together with the four queens for the last time at Castle Empyrean. Her sister had only been Queen of the Eastern Sky for about a week, but sitting at the table, Olena already looked different to her. The little girl still smiled and laughed like Zandria remembered, but now she seemed to radiate energy. Her smile instantly made Zandria smile back and her laughter gave Zandria a tingle all over. She guessed that Olena was quickly absorbing and learning how to use the powers of the queen.

They ate mostly in silence with the three older queens. Finished with the meal, Olena gestured to Tym. He came to her immediately and she whispered in his ear. Zandria tried to read her lips, but every time she focused on her sister's quietly moving mouth, her eyes would get watery. Zandria suspected Olena was using magic to help keep her secret. When the young queen finished speaking, Tym nodded without a word and moved to Zandria's chair. He scooted her away from the table and indicated for her to follow him out of the banquet hall.

Again, Zandria had the feeling of being ignored by the queens. She thought she had come to terms with their power and responsibilities. She told herself not to let it bother her and followed Tym along the ever transforming halls. She decided they had things to do and it most likely did not include her. It did not take long for Zandria to realize the elf was not taking her back to her room. Even though the castle did not share the secrets of its halls with her any longer, Zandria could tell when she was getting higher or lower. This morning, there was a lot of going upstairs.

Tym finally led her to a balcony that she knew all too well. He left her alone and Zandria stared down over the rail remembering saving Olena from falling on this very spot. This balcony was important to her because this is where she gave up the chance to become queen and instead saved her sister's life. Now, she knew it was not that difficult of a choice. She could not think of anything that mattered more to her than Olena.

Then Olena joined her. Being side-by-side, Zandria almost did not recognize her. Olena had not grown, but Zandria could feel the change in her. She seemed older.

Olena said, "You have a difficult path ahead of you."

This confused Zandria for two reasons. First, she did not know what her sister was talking about and second because her voice was not her own. It was as if Zandria was talking to an adult. There was a resonance to the little girl's voice that made Zandria not question her even though she did not understand.

"I'm not sure I'm supposed to be telling you this," Olena continued. "But you must make four into one, then what is lost shall be found."

Olena squeezed her eyes shut and scrunched up her face. Zandria knew this expression and called it Olena's Birthday Wish Face. When Olena opened her eyes, she looked like she had been asleep.

"Now what were you saying?" asked Olena in her little girl voice that Zandria knew and loved. Then came the "tsk" that she often punctuated her speech with. "That's right. You're going on a trip."

"But I'm not going any....." started Zandria. The sudden difference in her sister confused her even more. She suspected Olena did not even know she changed.

"Have fun and be safe," interrupted Olena. Then the young queen turned and skipped away.

Zandria tried to follow, but Tym reappeared and blocked the way.

He said, "Sometimes, Empyrean speaks through the queens. Mostly, it is to be ignored, unless the words have meaning for you." He paused. "Did they?"

"I don't believe so," said Zandria.

"Belief is a very powerful thing, positive or otherwise. I don't eavesdrop and did not hear what was spoken. I can tell you, though, sometimes they speak of the past and sometimes, the future. If it becomes clear, I am at your service. Otherwise, forget what was said," finished Tym.

Following the elf back to her bedroom, Zandria recounted Olena's words and she thought about her conversation with Fury from the other day. She wished again that she could find her mother's crystal. She wondered if the crystal was some kind of prison and if her mother was in pain. Zandria thought she was crying only because she was alone and scared. She hoped her mother was not hurt.

Alone in her bedroom, Zandria's thoughts turned from her mother trapped inside the crystal to how she might have been put there. She asked herself, did someone kidnap her? Was it one of the queens, maybe afraid of losing her throne? More likely, it was someone evil and the queens did not know how to break the spell. Zandria did not completely believe this because she saw the power of the four queens defeat the Forgotten Evil. She felt that freeing someone from a crystal prison should be easy for them.

Zandria's last thought before falling asleep that night was that the queens did not talk about it because they did not know what to do. She remembered Olena saying, in her trance, to make the four into one. Maybe, Zandria deduced, there was more than one crystal. If the queens did not have the other crystals, then there was probably nothing they could do. It made sense to Zandria that they would not want to talk about something that made them feel powerless. It also made her a little angry, but that feeling was drowned out by the snores coming from her little open mouth.

Continuous knocking awoke Zandria from her dreamless sleep. She was more disappointed in not dreaming than being waked in the middle of the night. Gradually becoming used to the cold glass floor night after night, Zandria went to the door barefoot. Not knowing whom to expect, she was a little surprised to find Tym on the other side.

"My apologies for this late hour. May I come in," he said.

Curious by his arrival, Zandria let Tym in and closed the door behind him. She sat on the edge of her bed and he stood in front of her.

"I was certain you would have sent for me by now," he continued. "All the same, I have something to show you. First, I have to explain."

Tym looked nervous, something she did not think the tall, slim elf could be. He wringed his hands, letting the pointed nails of his long, skinny fingers trace the back of each hand.

"I need to say that I do not risk any punishment as our queens are of a gentle nature. My worry is that I am going to tell you something that even their power cannot solve. As you already suspect, the Lost Queen and your mother are one in the same."

"I knew it," said Zandria. It made her feel better, though, to have someone tell her.

"With the recent passing of the Queen of the Eastern Sky, your mother should be the rightful queen. The magic of this place is unexplainable and unquestionable, and as such, your sister was called in your mother's place."

"And that has never happened before, right?" Zandria tried to show off her knowledge.

"Ever," said Tym. "Empyrean chooses its queens, not the people or heredity. The crux is that your mother is trapped and no one knows who did it or how to set her free."

"When she is free, what will happen to Olena?" asked Zandria.

"Your hope is inspiring and you assume much, but that is not for me to say. I do know that in my lifetime, there have never been two queens for the same throne and a new queen is never called until the previous queen has passed into the twilight."

"So why did you wake me up?" She wanted to know what he came to show her.

Tym knelt down to be directly in front of her. "Zandria, several days ago you spoke of finding the crystal. The queens were ashamed that they could not help your mother and hid the crystal, even from me. I know the castle wanted you to find it, but I do not know why. I have been contemplating this for these past nights and came to a decision. Tonight, I will take you to the crystal."

This confused Zandria, "You said you don't know where it's at."

"But you do," said Tym with an unexpected smile. "You said the room was behind a black door. As such, I said there is no Blackwood in this place. That type of wood comes from the Blackwood Forest in the far north. It is a place forbidden to my kind since the days of creation long before this castle grew from the dirt. When elves look upon Blackwood, they see nothing."

Beginning to understand, Zandria said, "So the queens hid the crystal right in front of you."

"For my protection, of course. The fewer that know the truth, the fewer that may fall victim to it. We do not know the extent of its power, but since it is your mother, I have decided to take you to her."

"You still don't know where the crystal is," said Zandria.

"All I have to do is look into the heart of Empyrean and see what I do not see," he said. Tym closed his eyes and bowed his head. This did not make sense to Zandria. After a moment, he looked at her and said, "I know."

Tym got to his feet and dashed to the hall. He looked in both directions to make sure it was clear. Then Zandria saw a look of concern slide across his face.

He said, "I will wait in the hall while you dress. Take anything you think you need, because you might not be coming back here."

She dressed quickly without another word. Zandria skipped past the dresses to find a simple shirt and short-legged pants. Then she opened the top drawer of her dresser. Next to the Glass Key of Soria Moria lay the knife given to her by the Prismata. She tucked it into her waistband, momentarily thinking about those rainbow princesses hidden beneath the waterfall. Then she joined Tym in the hall. If he could not see Blackwood, as he called it, she wondered how he knew where to go. She decided to follow him and see.

They moved quickly through the dark halls. Tym stopped occasionally to make sure no one would see them. It amused Zandria to see him press his back flat against the wall and crane his skinny neck around a corner, his braids swinging as he moved.

Neither of them spoke since leaving the room, so it startled Zandria when Tym said, "We should be close."

Zandria did not recognize the hallway, but the door was unmistakable when Tym walked past it. She knew he really could not see it.

"This is it," she said, pressing a hand against the glistening surface. The original chill returned, racing up her arm and through her body.

Tym's face looked as blank as the wall he must be seeing. Zandria tried to imagine not being able to see it, but could not get the oily sight out of her head. She opened the door and Tym's expression turned to a look of awe. She wondered if this was the first time he had ever seen the crystal.

Her concern for his experience diminished when she got close enough to touch it. This time, Zandria picked the crystal up without hesitation. Tym moved in for a closer look.

Zandria saw only the smoke moving inside, but Tym said, "Is that your mother?"

She turned the crystal around to see her mother on Tym's side and her heart leapt. The woman looked outward, but not at Zandria. It was as if she was looking at someone else.

Then her mother said, "Follow the crystal, Adam. You must help me."

Tym turned to Zandria and she saw his stunned surprise. She felt stunned too, but held back her shock. When she looked back to the crystal, her mother was gone.

Zandria knew without a doubt that wherever Adam was, he was holding another crystal at this same moment. Although she did not have her sister's abilities, Zandria could feel Empyrean's power within her. After hearing her mother's words now and Olena's from this morning, she knew what she had to do. Castle Empyrean wanted her to find the Lost Queen.

"I guess I'm going on a trip," said Zandria.

Without questions, Tym led Zandria down to the stables where they both explained everything to Fury. At first, the horse was groggy from sleep, but he was fully awake by the time they finished recounting the events.

Tym concluded, "Our reasoning from the information we have gathered is that there are four crystals. Between Zandria and her young friend Adam, we believe we hold two. Because of the nature of the door hiding this crystal, I feel there may be more answers in Blackwood Forest. If we can get Zandria to my clan in the Northern Wood, they can take her the rest of the way."

"I will do what I can, but I cannot leave my queen," offered Fury. "Instead, I'll have Tihi take you. She is absolutely trustworthy, but she can't speak." Fury nudged a young black mare sleeping by the few remaining Friesians. He looked back at Zandria and whispered with a smile, "Try not to rub it in though."

Zandria helped Tym saddle Tihi while Fury gave her instructions. Then the elf disappeared and returned shortly with some food to stock the saddlebags. Tihi knelt for Zandria to mount her. Tym and Fury walked them to the gate.

Tym said, "I will say your goodbyes for you. You will not be in any kind of trouble, but you know the queens could never give you permission for something they do not admit exists." She thought about this. When she realized that she made it to the castle on her own, she believed she could rescue her mother on her own.

"Watch that crystal for anymore messages," said Fury. "If Adam returns, we'll send him after you."

Tym added, "Somehow, I feel their paths will cross without our assistance. Farewell, Zandria."

"Be careful," said Fury to Zandria. She only nodded to them, intent on her quest. Then Fury said to Tihi, "Well? Get going girl."

Tihi galloped away into the night with Zandria holding tightly to the reins, praying not to fall.

Chapter 4

An Unwanted Duty

The basket ride to the top took longer than Adam liked. He hoped he would never see these horrible mines again and this final ascent was taking too long. He realized it was easier to lower the pulley contraption than it was for horses or men to raise it back to the top. Still, he needed them to go faster.

Finally, they were almost there. Adam could smell the fresh air and feel the warmth of the tropical sun. Then, with less than twenty feet to go, the basket suddenly stopped.

William looked concerned. He wrapped his hands around his eyes to block the sun as he peered toward the opening above them.

He said, "Something's not right."

Adam agreed silently. In his agitation, he looked over the fragile rail into the darkness below. The basket suddenly dropped a few feet and jolted to a stop. Adam pushed the thought of falling as far from his mind as he could. However, the image of himself and William smashed in the wreckage below would not leave his head.

The basket was going to fall, Adam told himself. He knew it instantly and said, "We can't stay on this thing."

"I concur," replied William. "Something is amiss above and we must not wait here to find out the cause."

Together Adam and William grabbed for the solid rocks jutting out of the wall. It only took a moment for Adam to find a footing and begin climbing. Again, his mind tumbled back to the day when the evil snail creature, General Gusk, sent him on his mission to stop Zandria and Olena. His hands and feet were strangely comfortable in repeating the experience of clawing his way out of the mines. He remembered being very near to this same height when he finally decided he was not going to follow his orders. He became determined to do what he could to stop the bad people who stole so much of his life and happiness. Of course, at that point, he had no idea how much his life would change.

Now, Adam remembered feeling extremely alone on this wall. Thankfully this day, that was different. Today, William hung next to him, clinging for his life. Despite their precarious position, Adam felt relieved to have this new friend with him. If they fell together, he thought somehow it might hurt less.

As they climbed closer to the surface, Adam could hear shouting. The inflection was urgent, but he could not make out the words. Then there was a loud cracking sound and an instant later, the pulley frame dropped past them. The frame, basket and lengths of rope disappeared into the darkness below. It fell so far that, even without the noise from above, he could not hear it hit the bottom. Feeling the rush of air as the wreck fell made Adam sick to his stomach. If the wood or rope had been any closer to the wall, it would have knocked him or William, or both of them, down with it. Sweat formed on the palms of his hands. Every second that he held still, he could feel his wet fingers slipping off the rock.

He concentrated on the sounds above him as he and William moved up slowly. Before they climbed out of the hole, the noises faded. The terrible and slow climb gave Adam more time for his eyes to adjust to the late morning sunlight. What he saw when he stood on the edge made him wish he was still in the darkness. Almost all of the men and horses that came with them were dead. Worse still, many of the bodies were small, like children.

"A wicked battle was fought above our heads only moments ago," said William. The prince stated the obvious, but there was no sign of the attackers.

Adam surveyed the courtyard and gateway. That is when he saw the bodies of the enemy that he originally mistook for children. There were a few children on the ground, but now he realized most of the smaller ones were dwarves.

"This must have been Lord Vanril's clan," said Adam.

"You mean the dwarves that led the Rockhorns against us?" asked William.

"Yes, these were his mines. But why wait until after we saved the others?"

"It is possible that they were only now returning or maybe they were in hiding, waiting to punish us," said William. "We did thoroughly hand it to them and they seem the type keen for revenge. I pray our brave men have defeated them for good and final today."

Adam looked around some more while William stopped to help a wounded soldier. Then there was a noise from the palace and a group of short people charged from their hiding spot. Before Adam realized it was the surviving slave children, he had his small sword drawn. The children surrounded him and William. They were followed closely by Humboldt. Adam noticed his blue uniform was dirty and he had a nasty looking slash across his left thigh. The moles Humboldt had become friendly with were nowhere to be seen.

"I tried to fight. I tried to save them," Hum rambled. He looked in shock.

William comforted him, "You did your best, my boy."

This struck Adam as odd to hear Prince William call Hum a boy. A few days ago, it would have sounded normal, but today William looked younger than Hum. Adam thought briefly about William's problems with his clothes not fitting right and started to understand what was happening.

"You protected the children," continued William. "The soldiers did their part and I do not think we have anything further to worry about."

"There is one problem," corrected Adam. "I don't see Vanril's body. He may not have an army now, but I don't think he's finished. He's not here."

This thought seemed to worry William a little, but the expression was not convincing on his boyish face. Adam was not sure if this would be a good time to point out that William was still getting younger. The Prince assured everyone that his reverse aging would stop when he was back to his natural age. Now, Adam was not so sure that was true. That seemed to be the least of their worries though.

William said, "We do not have the time to worry about one dwarf. We have too many tasks before us already. Not the least of which is tending to these wounded soldiers or finding the families of these children."

By the time they were finished cleaning wounds and clearing the courtyard, Adam counted their party of fifty reduced to nine including himself, William and Hum. Three of the four remaining Northerners turned out to be brothers. They were the three youngest of nine in the Smoltz family. A gardener from the West also survived, but Hum told William he did not know him personally. Aleta, the female crocodile rider, did not seem to be hurt, but only knelt silently next to her dying beast.

It appeared that the dwarves took the fiercest part of their attack to the animals. Aside from defeating the massive crocodile, they were left with only five Friesians. Adam was relieved to find Kalis and Sulis guarding the front entrance.

Inside the Palace by the Sea, they found food and soft beds for the children to sleep. While the little ones napped, the rest formed their plans. Adam watched as William naturally took the lead, but Terg tried to assert himself. Terg was the fourth surviving northerner that was not one of the three brothers. He had the hard look of being a lifelong soldier. Adam suspected he only recently experienced real fighting with the return of the Forgotten Evil.

"We need to stop Vanril before he gathers more forces against us," said Terg, leaning across the table where they were going to make their plans.

"I do not disagree, but our first duty is to the safety of these children," countered William.

"You are from the East," said Terg. "I do not expect you to know the bloodlines of the dwarves. Defeating Lord Vanril is a matter of honor that we owe to our countrymen."

William looked to be getting angry as Adam watched the debate continue. Both men stood face to face as if they were going to fight each other. With William's continual deaging, Adam thought it looked more like a father and son arguing than two leaders of an army. He did not want to see them hurt each other.

"You are right. I do not know of the bad blood that has arisen in your land," said William. "In my day, the ten families were as one under the rule of a great northern queen."

Terg seemed ready to strike, "Are you saying my queen is not great?"

Then Aleta stepped between them. With a strong accent, she said, "Enough. The children are behaving better than you two. Let us not forget them."

Adam could see the fire in her eyes. Aleta was a tall, muscular woman, but he could see her strength came from her heart. She had, so far, proven to be of very little words. Adam discovered that when she spoke, it carried great weight. He watched both William and Terg quickly regain their composure under her gaze. Even Hum and the gardener, Reinholdt, took a few steps back from the table.

William spoke first, "Forgive me, friend. These are trying times."

"Me as well. I will concede to the wisdom of my elders," said Terg with a smile. The joke of William's confusing age broke the tension and caused everyone to laugh, including a slight smile from the otherwise stoic Aleta.

Adam liked William's assertiveness. He wanted to have the same presence, inspiring people without looking down on them.

Spreading a map across the table, William explained, "We found several scrolls underground indicating the birthplaces of many of the young ones. Judging from the documents in this palace, many of those towns were lost to the wasteland."

Studying the map, Adam saw that much of it had been redrawn. Different color inks showed the gradual changes as the dwarves mined under the towns and villages of the East. Most of the map was inked in black and showed everything from the Palace by the Sea to the edge of the Euphoric Mountains. William read the names aloud, which made Adam thankful and a little frustrated at his own illiteracy. On the coast near the palace was the village of Banookanook. That made Adam momentarily think of Zandria. He wanted badly to tell her of the crystal he found.

Green ink traced the boundaries of the wasteland where the poisoned Royal Forest eventually sank into the ground. Across this massive area, too many red X's indicated the demise of the eastern townships. Adam saw only three other towns on the entire map that had not been crossed out of existence. He knew he had been to two of those when William read their names, Edge Town and Bremen. The third town was far to the south, near the edge of the map. His heart leapt into his throat when he heard the name Bond. He hoped this might be his home.

"We know what to expect in these other places," said William. "Bond is not a town I'm familiar with, but more than a few children come from there, including our good friend Adam."

Terg said, "That's on the other side of the Great Cliffs. Do you plan on carrying all of the little ones yourself?"

Adam thought the soldier was trying to challenge William again, but he had a good point. So, Adam said, "I know a way around."

William looked sad and hesitant. He said, "That information will be helpful, but I'm afraid you won't be coming with us."

"What are you talking about?" Adam felt his face flush red. He could not imagine William keeping him from a chance at finding his family.

"You have found something that needs to be returned to Castle Empyrean. I believe it is important, at the very least, to Zandria," said William. "If the message was true, then you must have some urgency. We will see to the safety of the refugees and I will not delay in finding your home."

"Maybe that's where I'm supposed to go," pleaded Adam. The crystal had yet to give him any more signs. Right now, his own mother meant more to him than Zandria's.

As genuine as he could sound, William insisted that Adam could not go with them. He added, "Remember, your instructions are to follow the crystal."

Adam grabbed the crystal from his waistband and tossed it on the table. It rolled sideways across the center of the map still open there. He said, "I don't care what it said. I'm going to find my family."

Then the crystal began to glow. As it grew brighter, black smoke twisted up in thin ribbons where the crystal singed the parchment beneath it. William tried to grab it, but yanked his hand back quickly, apparently feeling a burn from the now white shard.

Adam watched as the crystal began to slide across the map. It seared a line from the Palace by the Sea over the north edge of the wasteland and into what William called the Ice Caps. At the same time, he felt it burning into his heart. The burning sensation meant he realized there was a difference between what he wanted to do and what he had to do.

"That is where the frozen north meets the beginnings of the Euphoric Mountains," explained William. "On the other side of that is the queendom of the Northern Wood."

"Vexwood Forest," added Terg. "Even I wouldn't go there."

Adam was angry and confused. He wanted to feel like he was going home and at the same time he did not want to let down Zandria. He did not fully understand his feelings for her, but he had a sense that they might grow into something more over time. The woman in the crystal told him what to do. Now that he had the sign, Adam knew in his heart he had to follow it, despite his own desires.

"I understand," he said. "The rest of you have to take the children to Bond. There's too many of them for so few of you. I will follow the crystal, if you don't mind Kalis coming with me."

William put both hands on Adam's shoulders, then he let go for a moment to catch his pants before they sagged again. When he turned his attention back to Adam, he said, "You have my word that I will seek out your family. There is honor in doing your duty. That will make you a great man. Realize that we may not find anything when we get there, but you already have a new family. Keep that in your mind and heart."

Adam did not want to cry in front of the others. He fought back the urge because he believed William's promise. He hoped there would be a family waiting for him in Bond after he followed this crystal shard. He believed the best thing would be for him and Zandria to both have their mothers back.

The next morning, preparations were made for the party to separate. Saddled with extra supplies, Adam sat atop Kalis, watching the others head south. William, on Sulis, led with Hum and Reinholdt sharing a saddle. Aleta mounted a Friesian and the three young Smoltz Brothers moved on foot, corralling the excited group of children. Riding the fifth Friesian, Terg closed in the rear.

Adam hoped they would find people still living in Bond. He hoped they would find *his* mother. He gave William the instructions for heading southwest out of Banookanook. The path through the jungle would lead them to the waterfall along the edge of the Great Cliffs where he tracked the girls not too long ago. He watched this new parade dip out of sight below the rock wall marking the boundary of Banookanook.

"Let's go, Kalis."

"I looked at the map," said Kalis. "We could save time cutting across the wasteland."

"No good," said Adam. "There are too many sinkholes. Besides, there's a reason we're supposed to follow the crystal."

Adam liked the Friesian's initiative, but honestly thought they should follow the map as close as possible. Adam patted Kalis on his neck and they began making their way along the rocky coastline.

Chapter 5

Today's Weather, Rainy

Tihi was a fast horse, but she was gentle. When they bolted away from the castle, Zandria feared for her life. She thought for an instant that she would be bounced from the saddle and dropped into the waiting canyon surrounding the castle. Now that they were on the North Road, the Friesian found her full stride and it was smooth. The gentle rocking of the gallop made it easy for Zandria to fall asleep.

The morning sun from the west woke Zandria early. She could not believe that she did not fall off Tihi's back during the night. It amazed her that the horse kept her rider intact at such a fast gallop. The unusual bed left Zandria with peaceful dreams of gliding across the plains.

Now, all she could see was the tall, thick grass that surrounded Castle Empyrean in every direction. Zandria could not see the castle behind her or her destination ahead of her. She thought they must have covered an incredible distance during the night. She tried to imagine the approaching Northern Wood, but her only experience with trees came from the tropical palms of Banookanook or the rotting, gnarled trees of the Dead Forest. She did not know what to expect.

Zandria's thoughts turned back to Tihi. She did not realize the endurance of the Northern Friesians. She spent so little time with both Fury and Wrath during her last journey that she never saw their true magnificence. Tihi seemed to have great stamina. She galloped for the entire day without breaking stride. Zandria did not even leave the saddle, eating lunch where she sat. The horse and rider continued on after it was too dark to see that night. Finally, Zandria became too sore from sitting in the saddle. She hoped Tihi wanted to stop for the night.

When the horse slowed to a walk on the side of the road, Zandria said, "Thank you, dear Tihi." She knew she was not completely in charge of this expedition and did not expect a response, but added, "This looks like a great spot to camp for the night."

Tihi stamped a hoof in apparent agreement and then settled down on the side of the road. After the Friesian knelt, Zandria found it easy to climb off. She quickly unrolled a blanket next to the resting mare. When she settled, she pulled a heavy brush from one of the saddlebags and began stroking Tihi's mane.

She said, "Forgive me for not removing the saddle, but I would not know how to put it back on."

Tihi neighed and Zandria took that as a sign of understanding. A little while later, without a campfire or dinner, she fell asleep. Zandria felt secure nestled against Tihi's soft hair.

Her dream came easy that night and again she was gliding over the Great Plains. Zandria looked beneath her to see that she was flying. She could not see Tihi or anyone else. She raced along enjoying the breeze on her face without any concerns.

Then smoke started to rise from the grass. It danced around her, but the sky was still clear above her. Fully aware that she was dreaming, Zandria did not worry about the smoke at first. She thought maybe there was a wild fire left over from the Rockhorn battle, but she saw no light or felt no heat. Still without much concern, she sailed on over the grass.

Gradually, the smoke grew thicker. It started closing in to where she could reach out to touch it. Her fingers left little wispy trails in the air as she brushed the wall-like mists. Soon, the smoke completely surrounded her. She could no longer see stars above or grass below her. Even this did not worry her until she felt herself slowing.

Zandria finally stopped moving and her feelings grew in small bursts from concern through fear to panic. Even in her panic, she did not lose control because she knew this was a dream. However, she did not like the sensation of simply hanging in midair. She could not feel anything holding her up, like the sensation when her father used to pick her up under her arms to spin her around. Zandria tried waving her arms too, but she did not move anywhere because this was not like floating in water either. She could not swim to safety. She also kicked her feet, trying to reach the ground, but futilely ran in place.

Finally, Zandria realized where her dream had taken her.

She spoke aloud in a dreamy echo, "I'm inside the crystal."

That is when her mother appeared to her out of the mist.

"My child," said her mother, "why do you move without thinking?"

"What do you mean?" asked Zandria. She could barely see her mother. Shrouded in the mist, she thought the woman might also be floating.

"You go north without knowing your destination," responded her mother.

"Tym said Blackwood Forest could hold another crystal," answered Zandria. She did not hesitate to tell her mother the truth.

"Blackwood is not the only forest in the Northern Wood," explained the woman.

"Where should I go then?" asked Zandria.

Zandria thought her mother looked like she knew something she was not saying. The woman answered her question with, "This is your dream, sweet Zandria. I can only tell you what you already know."

"But I don't know anything," Zandria complained. The mysterious answers started to frustrate her.

"You know Adam has one of the crystals and you know your sister told you there are only four. Let the boy that you trust find another to ease your burden. When you find the one you seek, you will be reunited with your friend," finished her mother. This seemed like a more complete answer, but it still confused her.

"Then you will be free," said Zandria, trying to get to the point.

"These crystals are much more than a prison. And you already suspect there are evil beings seeking this power."

Zandria's mother faded into the smoke, leaving Zandria alone again. Then the gray cloudiness around her was washed away by a sudden rain shower. In an instant, Zandria was soaked. She awoke to discover the rain was not only in her dream.

Already awake, Tihi waited patiently for Zandria. As Zandria became aware of her surroundings, Tihi turned to her and said, "Get on child. We should try to get to the cover of the wood before this storm gets worse."

Zandria did not move. She thought maybe she was still dreaming and said, "But Fury said...I mean...you can't talk."

"What I cannot do and what I do not do are two different things. Being a mare in a stallion's army is not easy. It is hard enough to stay on even hoofing without the sound of my voice being a constant reminder," said Tihi.

"Are they prejudiced?" Zandria did not have much experience with it, but she knew sometimes people did not like others only because they were different. It surprised and disappointed her that this might happen with animals too.

"Let me put it this way," explained Tihi. "The Friesians would much rather see me suckling a colt than leading a charge. Now let's keep this as our secret and get you on before we sink into the mud or drown."

Zandria climbed onto the slippery saddle and Tihi stood. Then they splashed onto the North Road. Through the downpour and pale morning light, Zandria could make out what seemed to be a high wall in the distance. This must be the border to the Northern Wood, she thought. Knowing they would be there soon enough was a relief because her mind was still reeling at Tihi's vocal revelation. She started to shiver from the wet cold.

When they got closer, Zandria saw that it was not exactly a wall, but only a line of trees. The trees, however, were bigger than any she had ever seen. She was used to the palms by the beach that she could wrap her arms around, climb up and grab a piece of fruit. The trees here were so wide that she guessed it would take ten of her to reach all the way around them. They were so tall that she would not even want to try to climb to the green covered branches far above her.

The hard downpour already slowed to a peaceful drizzle. The sun tried to cut through the clouds, slightly warming things. Passing between the trees on the North Road at a slower pace, Zandria noticed a small stone engraved with the words "Welcome to the Northern Woods. Today's weather – rainy, turning to sun in the afternoon."

Zandria asked Tihi, "Does someone carve a new stone every day?"

Before Tihi answered, a new line of words appeared on the stone beneath the greeting. It read, "No, I'm a magic stone, thank you very much."

This brought a smile to Zandria's face. She liked the idea of being in a land that was so magical that even the rocks were friendly. It was definitely a nice change from the unfriendly Rockhorns.

A few paces past the wall, the rain stopped entirely. Zandria looked back at the plains to see it still coming down quite heavily in the distance. Now surrounded by countless trees, the millions of thirsty leaves over her head absorbed the fading rain.

"This is Greatwood Forest," said Tihi, now moving at a much slower gait.

"It's beautiful. I've never seen anything like it," said Zandria. The unexpected sound of the Friesian's voice still seemed unfamiliar, but she was glad to have someone to talk to.

As she looked at the thick, knotty roots digging deep into the ground, Tihi continued, "These are the tallest and oldest trees in all of the six forests that make up the Northern Wood."

"There are six forests like this?"

"No other like this, but yes, six," answered Tihi. "A millennia ago, the first Queen of the Northern Wood united the six separate forests under one rule. When Snow White became queen, she tried to give the lands back to their people and elected a governor for each forest. In my lifetime, I've watched the territories slowly grow apart and become isolated from each other."

"But they're still loyal to the queen, right?" asked Zandria. Every new land she explored fascinated her.

"So they say, but, as you know, only the Friesians and men of Castlewood fought against the Rockhorn army. There are many other people in the Northern Wood and we are still days away from the stable I call home," said Tihi.

"You live in Castlewood Forest? That must be where Snow White's castle is," said Zandria.

"It was not always hers," explained Tihi. "They say the forest grew up around that castle. It has been home to many different queens, kings, princesses and princes. As well as many different curses."

"Curses?" Zandria was curious.

Tihi stopped in her tracks. "Tym did not tell you, I see. That's why I do not trust elves, they tend to be a deceitful people. The Northern Wood is full of curses, although those that created them are long gone. They say that one time everyone in the castle was put to sleep because a girl cut her finger on a sewing wheel. Sometimes, I think humans purposely invent new ways to get into trouble."

"We've never had anything like that where I'm from." The conversation was beginning to make Zandria nervous. First, she never suspected Tym of trying to trick her, but Tihi was pretty definite. Maybe Tym knew more about the crystal than he could say within Empyrean, she thought. The queens probably did not want him to talk about it. That must be why he sent her to the other elves.

Then she thought more about the curses. This started Zandria looking all around her. She did not want a curse falling on her. She saw the massive trees were so wide and so closely spaced that it was more like traveling in a cave than a forest. She feared there could be anything hiding close, but completely out of sight. She had no idea what could be in the surrounding forest. She thought curses might be something simple like spoken words, but Tihi talked about them like they were animals.

Zandria quickly decided it was better not to worry about that and turned her mind to being in a new country. She wanted to know more about the Northern Wood and asked, "What are the names of the other forests?"

"Greatwood, as you have seen, guards the southern edge of our land and stretches almost to the Euphoric Mountains," said Tihi. "Castlewood and Truewood are near the central valley. You will see Truewood in a few days because that is where the elf clan lives which we are going to see."

Zandria interrupted, "And I know Blackwood is to the north."

"That is a treacherous journey which I do not look forward to," continued Tihi.

"What are the names of the other two?" asked Zandria, trying not to think of possible trouble yet to come.

"To the west is Peckwood. That is a land of strange creatures and very few humans. Lastly, to the far east, bordering on the mountains, is Vexwood," said Tihi.

At that, Tihi fell silent and Zandria was impressed by the consuming quiet around her. There were no animals or birds that she could see or hear. Zandria sighed at the emptiness. Tihi must have anticipated Zandria's coming boredom and said, "Why don't you tell me about yourself."

For the remaining days on the road to Castlewood, Zandria told Tihi about everything she could. She talked about Banookanook and the Palace by the Sea. She made sure to include Kez and the quzzaks. Then she told of the attack on the Queen of the Eastern Sky and her and Olena's trip to Empyrean. It especially interested Tihi the time Fury encountered the unicorns. Zandria thought she detected a little jealousy, so she tried to emphasize his bravery when he rescued them in Bremen.

The talking helped Zandria pass the time and she felt like her and Tihi were old friends when they arrived at the northern castle.

They crossed an open field to enter the castle gate. She expected at least some kind of town surrounding the castle, but saw nothing. It excited her too much to finally be at the castle that she did not give another thought to any possible town.

"Please remember not to talk to me in front of anyone," said Tihi as a pair of Friesians came out of the castle to greet them. Zandria did not want to betray the trust of her new friend. She did not think it would matter if Tihi could talk, but she would not be the one to reveal it.

The two strong black stallions were followed by a group of five dwarves. Zandria recognized the one in the lead from their recent victory at Castle Empyrean. She remembered Wrath calling him Professor Erbadin, the head of the seven dwarven families.

Professor Erbadin bowed to Zandria and his beard touched the dirt. "We've been expecting you," said the ancient dwarf.

Caught off guard by his comment, Zandria quickly realized that one of the tiny Guardian Hawks from Castle Empyrean could easily have delivered a message. The small bird could fly faster than Tihi could gallop and take a more direct course. It surprised her that any of the four queens would acknowledge her mission, since they would not even talk to her about it.

When Professor Erbadin said, "I am ashamed that my Royal Highnesses feel the need to inspect my work," Zandria understood that no one here knew her true quest.

"Please don't be offended," said Zandria, thinking quickly. She recalled that Professor Erbadin and his artisans were tasked with rebuilding the drawbridge that was destroyed in the attack on Castle Empyrean. "No one doubts your skill. I requested a tour of your beautiful country. I was not sent here only to check on you. My sister, the Eastern Queen, was simply curious of your progress."

This answer seemed to satisfy Professor Erbadin. She must have guessed correctly that he received a message and what it was about. He said, "Very well. Welcome to Castlewood Castle." Then he gave another beard-dirtying bow and Zandria wondered how his facial hair ever stayed clean.

Zandria dismounted Tihi and the mare left with the other Friesians to refresh in the stables. Zandria walked with the dwarves, feeling like she towered over them. Inside the castle, they fed her a generous meal and Erbadin elaborated on the new bridge.

"We have only completed the selection of the adequate timber in Greatwood," he said. Amused by the small man sitting in a human sized chair, Zandria barely paid attention to his words. "The first of the trees is scheduled to be felled tomorrow. Once all of the wood is cut and sanded, we are going to attempt a new technique. Some of our alchemists believe they have achieved a method of making the wood fireproof."

"Fascinating," said Zandria, stuffing another bite of crème cake in her mouth.

For being offended by the surprise inspection, Zandria thought the overworked dwarf was very thorough in his explanation. She suspected he was secretly proud of his work and could not wait to share it with anybody that would listen. Zandria decided she liked this Professor Erbadin.

Professor Erbadin kept her company the rest of the evening. He showed her to a bedroom with a blazing fireplace that stretched across one entire wall. Zandria thought the heat would be unbearable with as warm as it was outside.

"Take a deep breath," instructed Erbadin.

She did as she was told. Zandria inhaled a soothing scent of flowers. Then she realized there was a slightly cool breeze pushing the calming aroma into the room.

"Peckwood," explained Professor Erbadin. "It burns cooler than the other types of Northern wood. We use it in some medicines, but it's also great to help you sleep."

"Thank you, sir," said Zandria. The idea of a cold fire amazed her.

"You're quite welcome, my lady," responded Erbadin. "Incidentally, I could assign you a guide for the rest of your trip. My dwarves know every part of the lower forests."

Not wanting to give away her mission, Zandria said, "I think Tihi will do nicely. By the way, what do you mean lower forests?"

"The five lower forests. No one ventures north of the old mines to Blackwood."

"Too bad," said Zandria. "I heard Blackwood was worth seeing."

"Tihi may be mute, but even she knows not to take you there," said Professor Erbadin. "She'll take you round to Peckwood and Truewood. I would be happy to send along someone who could tell you the stories and history of the area."

"That is not necessary," said Zandria. "I trust Tihi completely." She did not want to give away Tihi's secret either.

"As you wish. Until then, have a pleasant sleep," said Erbadin. He looked reluctant to leave her with those arrangements. She hoped he would not push the issue in the morning.

The dwarf left the room and Zandria settled into bed. She lay on her side, staring into the dancing flames of the biggest fireplace she had ever seen. The gentle breeze of cool scented air did calm her. Zandria fell asleep before she could put any thought to the coming journey, the crystal, the elves or Blackwood Forest.

Chapter 6

New Friends Along the Way

They were only a day away from the Palace by the Sea. Adam and Kalis had been following the rocky, brown shoreline due north as the crystal instructed. So far, the journey had been uneventful. The closest the boy and horse came to another living thing since they left was a lonely seagull. Busy cracking the shell of something it plucked from the sea, the bird paid them no mind.

The horse spoke, "That makes me somewhat hungry."

Still watching the bird peck at the chewy flesh inside the shell, Adam said, "Ugh. That makes you hungry?" It did not look at all appealing to him.

"Not that per say. I've never been one for seafood. It's more the concept of stopping for a mid-day meal that intrigued me," replied Kalis.

Adam looked from the edge of the jungle to the splashing water of the ocean. The only things between the water and the jungle besides the seagull were the small, jagged rocks. He did not look forward to sitting on the sharp ground after riding in this hard, leather saddle all morning. When they camped last night, they were lucky enough to find a small clearing on the edge of the jungle. Both he and the Friesian slept on sun-warmed sand. For no good reason, Adam did not think their luck would hold today.

Then, in the distance, Adam spotted a wide flat rock sticking up from the shore. He pointed it out to Kalis and the horse carefully made his way across the uneven ground.

"This should be good. We can rest her for a bit," said Adam.

He examined the rock. It was smooth, almost like glass, and wide enough to hold them both, plus a few others if anyone had been with them. Also, Adam noticed this rock was darker than the rest. Instead of the dull reddish-brown, it was black with silver speckles.

When Kalis stepped up onto the rock, Adam realized how high it stuck up over the beach and one edge poked out over the lapping waves. As Adam dismounted and began digging in his bags for food, he felt the spray as the ocean slapped against the side of the rock below him. Adam knew this rock came from somewhere else, but sitting on the cool surface and relaxing, he stopped wondering about its origin. Being elevated made it the ideal spot for a seaside picnic and that satisfied him.

Before they finished eating, the lonely seagull joined them. It started pecking at some dropped breadcrumbs as Adam studied its mix of gray and white feathers. Adam looked into the large bird's eyes and saw only his own face reflected in the black pupils. He noticed one of the bird's wings had a knot on it at the top edge. Adam guessed the wing bone had been broken at one time. He tried to guess if the bird was male or female, but did not know birds well enough. Besides, it did not say anything yet and he hoped the sound of its voice would make it clear. Instead, the seagull sat silently waiting for Adam to drop another bite.

When they were finished resting, Kalis stood up first. This startled the bird and it quickly fluttered to the far edge of the rock. Crumb, as Adam decided to nickname the seagull, sat there watching him pack the remaining food. In an effort to be kind, Adam tore off one last chunk of bread and tossed it. Crumb quickly flapped his wings and caught the morsel in midair. Adam watched Crumb circle them twice and then swoop out over the water. He thought that would be the last he would see of the lonely bird.

With Adam back in the saddle, they began heading north again. Adam figured they still had at least another day before they reached the point where the crystal instructed them to turn west across the wasteland. They did not see any other seagulls that day.

"I suggest we do not stop for the night until we find another adequate space," said Kalis as the sun started to set beyond the sea.

Adam thought about the hollow spot at the edge of the jungle from last night and then thought about other possibilities. "We should watch for more big rocks," he said. There was something about that black rock from earlier that intrigued him.

"That is unlikely," said Kalis without further explanation.

Adam verbally prodded him, "What makes you so sure?"

Kalis did not answer at first. After negotiating three careful steps over some particularly precarious rocks, he said, "That rock did not belong there."

Adam understood and that gave him a strange feeling. Somehow, he, too, knew that rock did not belong there. He saw no other rock like it since they had been on this shoreline. Also, he never encountered any similar stones in his years underground. He knew it was not natural. This made him want to know more about it, though.

"Where do you think it came from?" he asked.

"I don't," said Kalis.

"What does that mean?" asked Adam. He felt like Kalis maybe knew something about it.

"It means there are some things that one must accept. I did not put the rock there, I cannot move it and I don't know where it came from. It *is* and that's *that*," said Kalis.

Adam was disappointed with the answer. He knew now that Kalis was not going to elaborate and probably, in actuality, knew nothing more. Sometime later, Adam would learn the truth about that mysterious rock, but that is for another tale yet to come.

Kalis added, "Don't worry about things you cannot change."

The Friesian changed the subject and this new statement had a deep impact on Adam. The words resonated in his head. Most of his life, he concerned himself only with digging and pounding at rocks. Since coming above ground, he helped Olena become queen and led a rescue party to save the rest of the children in the mines. He wondered if saving an entire queendom was something he should worry about normally. Kalis' words made sense, but he felt like it took a lot of the excitement out of life. He knew his worry about stopping Vanril and General Gusk was necessary when he escaped. Then he realized the flat rock had no meaning for him now and he suspected he would never see it again. That was something he could not change.

To Kalis, he said, "Still, it's fun imagining."

That night, they found an inlet surrounded by dry sand and tucked back into the jungle. Adam unsaddled Kalis and they made camp. Both horse and boy bathed in the calm, salty water. Afterward, Adam made a small fire and they slept soundly.

In the morning, Adam woke to find a large seagull sleeping on the other side of the extinguished campfire. After a moment, the bird rustled awake. It stretched its wide wings and Adam saw the bony knot.

"Crumb!" he said.

The sound of Adam's voice roused Kalis from sleep. He bolted up in a defensive posture, then relaxed when he saw the bird.

Adam said again, "It's Crumb. He followed us."

"How do you know it's a *he*?" asked Kalis.

"I don't. It feels right, though," said Adam.

Kalis stomped the ground in front of the bird. Crumb did not stir this time. Adam did not want the horse to chase away the bird. The new company made him happy.

Kalis said, "It seems we have acquired a new traveling companion."

Crumb did not leave them at all that day. Occasionally, he would fly out over the ocean and snatch up a tiny fish. Then he would fly ahead and patiently wait for them on a random palm tree bent out over the beach. Other times, he would drop behind, then swoop past them.

At lunchtime, Crumb roosted right next to Adam. This time they found no comfortable spot. As Adam ate, he figured the seagull was only following them for the food. He did not believe Crumb was really a new friend.

Adam decided to pull the map out of the leather tube strapped to the saddle. He unrolled it to see their path still burned into the parchment like a black scar. He did not want to tell Kalis that he had no idea where they were.

"We have to be getting close," said Adam.

"Are there any landmarks?" asked Kalis.

"Land what?" asked Adam. He also did not yet want to tell Kalis that he could not read.

"Symbols on the map," explained the horse. "We have to match them up to the real world."

There was nothing on the map where they were supposed to turn. Adam recognized the picture of the Palace by the Sea and guessed the word below it indicated the village of Banookanook. There were no other symbols on the coastline all the way to the top of the map, not even the black rock. Adam grabbed the crystal and dropped it on the map, hoping it would move again.

Nothing happened.

Suddenly, Crumb flailed his wings and snagged the crystal. He flew away quickly and disappeared into the jungle only a short distance away.

"A beggar and a thief," said Kalis.

Adam did not believe that. He wanted to run after the bird, but paused. His suspicion was that Crumb was unknowingly leading them. He still hoped that Crumb was a friend and not simply a scavenger. Maybe, he thought, the crystal was controlling the bird. Adam did not understand its power, but thought that might be possible. Knowing he had to follow Crumb, Adam gathered up their things and quickly mounted Kalis.

"We have to go after him," Adam said.

When they made it to the spot where Crumb changed directions, Adam was only a little surprised to find a path leading into the jungle. The surrounding bushes and branches were cleared back and evenly cut on both sides. The sand floor was smooth and well packed. This trail was not nearly as frequently traveled as the Great Road, but, Adam thought, was maintained extremely well.

A few feet down the path, Crumb sat waiting on the ground. The crystal lay in the sand in front of him. When he saw Adam, he nudged the crystal towards him with his beak. Adam jumped down and grabbed the crystal. He was relieved, but swore never to let it out of his sight again. He did not think he could face Zandria if he lost it. Adam thought he might scold Crumb, but before he could, the seagull flew up into a nearby tree.

Back with Kalis, Adam examined the map again.

"If this trail is on the map, it has to be under the crystal's mark," said Adam. "Crumb was only trying to show us the way."

"You're lucky," said Kalis. "Where I come from, birds are notorious thieves of small items."

Adam said, "You have to be more trusting. Now, I know this is probably nothing to worry about, but who do you think made this road?"

Kalis shook his head and the shudder passed down his neck, through his body and out his tail. He said, "You are right that the maker of this road is of little importance. Our thought should be as to who recently cut back these plants."

He knew the path looked well cared for, but now Adam noticed the wet sap on the nearby branches. Someone had recently cut them back. Whoever it was, he hoped the caretaker turned out to be friendly. This too seemed like something he should not worry about, unless they actually met someone along the way.

Kalis carried Adam into the jungle. They spent one night on the path and got an early start the next morning. Kalis seemed disappointed to find Crumb still with them.

By the end of the next day, they came to a wide clearing at the edge of the wasteland.

Adam immediately felt the sting of guilt and responsibility at the sight of the devastated wastelands. He knew it was the mining he was forced to do that decimated this land. For some reason, it did not feel as painful to see when he was traveling with William. The Prince's confidence must have spilled over to him, he thought. He liked Kalis and Crumb, but they were mostly strangers and this suddenly made him feel alone facing the desolation. He did not know how he could ever repay the debt for his part in the destruction. However, he vowed he would try.

Now, he turned his attention back to the clearing, still lush and green. The wide lawns spread out on both sides of the path, but were easily as meticulous. On one side, a stone well poked out of the ground with a bucket resting on its lip. This immediately made Adam thirsty for some cool, fresh water. To the other side stood a single, metallic gray boulder. Adam wondered if this was going to be a journey for discovering new rocks. He had never seen a metallic looking stone before, either.

Suddenly, the boulder raised its head. Then it rolled back its shoulders and stretched out its arms. It took Adam until the thing was fully standing to realize the rock was actually a man. The metal man had been hunched over into a ball, but now stood to his full nine foot height.

As he turned and walked towards them, Adam saw that the metal covering his body was his skin. He was not wearing armor, but a sleeveless white shirt that showed off his immensely muscular arms. Seeing how the man also wore tan pants made Adam wonder how he could have thought it was a rock in the first place.

"He's made of metal," said Adam in dismay.

"Iron," said the man in a sullen voice. He must have heard the statement from across the lawn, Adam thought.

"What?" said Adam.

"Not metal. Iron. I am made of iron." The giant man's words came out slowly as if he had to think of them one at a time.

His long legs quickly moved the iron man next to them. As he came closer, Kalis stepped back. "This must be the caretaker," said the Friesian.

Crumb circled overhead, watching.

Adam definitely hoped this caretaker was friendly. He looked for a possibility of escape, in case he was not. However, he had the overwhelming feeling that this man could not be dangerous. He quickly decided on a new tactic.

"What's your name?" Adam asked, playing a hunch that he was about to make another new friend.

The man standing on the ground towered over the boy sitting on horseback. He looked down at them, confusion spreading across his face. Adam saw Crumb reflected in his shiny bald head.

With effort, the iron man said, "I don't remember. That's why I have this."

He reached toward his chest and pinched a small wooden sign with the thumb and forefinger of both hands. Adam did not notice it earlier, but there it hung, tied with rope hanging from his neck. There was a single word written on it, but Adam had no idea what it spelled.

Adam surmised with the man's great size and apparently slow ability to reason, it would not be a good idea to lie.

"Sorry, friend," he said. "I can't read."

Kalis neighed. Adam hoped the horse would not be angry with him for keeping this secret. He realized it did not matter now.

"Me can't neither," said the giant with an expression of defeat. Then his face lit up with a smile. He said, "Maybe horsy can tell it to us."

Kalis looked at the small sign for a moment. The he said, "Forgive me. I don't do well with human writing. I learned dwarven. Besides, this must be an eastern form. Maybe, Adam, when this is over, we can learn something new together."

Adam appreciated Kalis' offer. He never knew how important reading could be. He had no use for it in the mines, but now reading seemed to be one of the most important things he should know.

Crumb perched on the horn of the saddle. Adam thought for a moment that the bird was trying to read the nametag. He realized that was a silly idea since Crumb could not even talk. Then the bird took off and landed on the big man's head.

The seagull squawked, "Aye-ya-ha."

The bird had been helpful before. Maybe, Adam thought, he could read and was trying to tell them the name.

"I don't understand, Crumb," said Adam.

"Aye-ya-ha," came the squawk again.

This time Crumb pecked at the man's head with a clink, clink, clink.

"That tickles," said the man. He looked like he wanted to swat the bird away, but stopped himself with his arm half-raised.

Crumb fluttered down and landed on the man's bulging forearm. He repeated the maneuver from head to arm two more times, then sailed into the air. He let out the same sound again, "Aye-ya-ha."

"Well, I don't think it's Ayaha," said Adam. "It has something to do with his head and arm," he said to Kalis. Then to the giant, "Does that sound right?"

The iron man raised his enormous hand the rest of the way to the top of his head and scratched it with one finger. "I don't think so," he said.

"Maybe," suggested Kalis, "it's not the head, but what he's made of. Something such as Iron Arm."

Another squawk from above, "Aye-ya-ha."

The big man smiled again, "That's right birdie. Eisenhahn. How did you know?"

"Eisenhahn?" asked Kalis.

"I guess Crumb can read," said Adam. With the name said aloud, Crumb's squawking now sounded quite clear. It actually sounded like the bird said Eisenhahn. Adam stuck out a hand to Eisenhahn and said, "Pleased to meet you. I'm Adam." Gesturing to the Friesian, he added, "This is Kalis."

Their handshake felt funny because Adam could barely wrap his hand around one of Eisenhahn's fingers.

Adam shouted up to the seagull, "Good job, Crumb."

"Is it time to go back to work already?" asked Eisenhahn. He started to lumber towards the path.

Kalis must have understood what he meant. He said, "No, please. Don't go anywhere. The passage is in fine shape."

"Good. Master told me to always take care of it."

Adam wondered if there was someone else around. He thought the path must be for someone. "Is your master here?"

"What master?" asked Eisenhahn as if he had not mentioned it only moments before.

"Who do you tend the path for?" asked Kalis.

Eisenhahn thought about the answer for what seemed like too long, then said, "For you, I suppose."

"Well, what about before us?" asked Adam. "Does anybody else come this way?"

"Not anymore."

"Who used to?" pried Adam.

"Used to what?" came Eisenhahn's innocent reply.

This could easily become frustrating, Adam felt, so he tried to have patience. "Before us, who used to travel on your trail?"

"No one," said Eisenhahn. "Master said to keep it nice for a horsey, birdie and a boy that talked a lot. I guess they never came."

This stunned Adam. He could not believe this giant might purposely have been left here to wait for them. Even still, how could anyone have known that Crumb would be with them? He had no idea how long Eisenhahn had been tending the path either. What if he had been waiting hundreds of years, he asked himself.

Kalis seemed to understand the implication as well. He asked, "How did your master know about us?"

Eisenhahn did not seem to understand the question. Adam could tell from his expression that this was the end of the conversation and they would probably never know the answer.

After a moment, Eisenhahn broke the awkward silence with, "Are you thirsty? I'm thirsty."

The urge Adam felt earlier overcame his curiosity. They had been rationing their stale water since the Palace by the Sea and he wanted something cold. He remembered the well behind him and jumped down from Kalis. On the ground, he discovered he only stood as tall as Eisenhahn's knees. As amusing as that was, his dry mouth could not wait any longer. Without a word, he dashed to the well and looked down at the inviting water. Crumb landed on the side as Adam tossed in the bucket, being sure to hold onto the rope. The splash below made his mouth feel even drier.

He was already pulling up a full pail when Eisenhahn said, "Wait. You can't drink master's water."

"I think your master is long gone," said Adam. "So what's he gonna do?"

"Something bad," said Eisenhahn.

Afterwards, Adam wished he had listened. He took a sip, careful not to spill the entire bucket on himself. Almost as soon as he swallowed, he felt a strange numbness on the top of his head. His natural brown hair instantly turned to a bright shiny copper. Kalis neighed with surprise, but Adam did not understand what happened until he saw his reflection at the bottom of the well.

"Did my hair turn to metal?" he asked, touching it gently.

"Copper, to be precise," answered Kalis.

"I drank a whole bucket," said Eisenhahn.

"So, you weren't always made of iron?" asked Adam.

"I guess not."

Kalis stamped the ground. He looked, to Adam, like he was trying to stifle laughter. "It doesn't look that bad, actually."

Ignoring the Friesian, Adam asked, "Why would you offer us a drink, if you knew it was bad?"

Eisenhahn looked like Adam's scolding might make him cry. "I didn't. I asked if you had a drink because I was thirsty."

"I don't think anyone else should drink from it," said Kalis.

Adam turned back to dump out the bucket in time to see Crumb beak out a big gulp. He watched in amazement as the seagull transformed. His beak, legs and eyes went first. Then one by one in rapid succession, every gray and white feather turned to gold.

Chapter 7

Dew Lantisphere

Sometime during the night, the fire ended its frenzied dance. Now all that remained of the magical Peckwood was charred ashes. Zandria understood why Professor Erbadin said they used the wood in medicines. She awoke completely refreshed. She could not remember the last time she slept this well.

Zandria snuggled in her bed in a pleasant mood. She could feel an uncontrollable, dreamy smile on her face, but she did not want to open her eyes yet. She tried to remember last night's dream. When nothing came back to her, she let her mind drift to thoughts of her mother.

In her memory, her mother was like a queen. She was forever beautiful and always surrounded by warm, welcoming light. She barely knew her, but Zandria knew she loved that woman.

In the past few days, Zandria's thoughts became clouded by the images from the crystal. This woman was still beautiful, but she looked tired and worn. The childhood fantasy in her mind was replaced with this new reality. While she still felt love for her mother, she now saw her only as a person. She wondered, for an instant, if it would be better to have the memory instead of the reality. She quickly pushed that thought out of her head.

She knew there was one thing that a living, breathing body could give her that no memory could. Zandria wanted to be hugged. She had plenty of people that could do that, such as Olena, Adam or even one of the other queens. Yet, nothing could replace that ultimate feeling of comfort, security and sacred love that could only come from a mother. The sensation that consumed her was the gentle arms engulfing her body, pulling her close and lifting her from the ground. She was only four years old the last time she felt it and longed for it ever since.

Zandria kept her eyes closed now because they were filled with tears. She did not care what was waiting for her in Blackwood Forest or who controlled the crystals. Nothing could stop her from saving her mother. Nothing could take that hug away from her.

Soon the warm smell of baking bread replaced the fading scent of the Peckwood. Zandria pulled herself out of bed and dressed with a growing excitement. Other smells of cooking food began to mix with the aroma of the bread. She followed her nose to the castle's kitchen. There she found twelve of the busiest dwarven women she had ever seen.

The breakfast was not lavish, but it was hearty. Zandria ate her fill of fresh eggs scrambled with goat cheese and some type of green vegetable. Her drink was a sweet, sticky nectar that Professor Erbadin only referred to as "sap". She stood in the kitchen, picking at hot buttered rolls, until the meal was ready. When everything was moved into the dining hall, they were joined by more dwarves, including Erbadin, and some human soldiers.

Zandria leaned back in her chair, stuffed and feeling like she wanted to go back to bed. "Do you eat like this every day?" she asked.

"I couldn't imagine," answered Erbadin.

Zandria assumed they made this special meal for her.

Professor Erbadin continued, "We had to have a small breakfast because we need to get to work on the bridge."

The thought of this being a small breakfast shocked Zandria. She could not imagine eating more or having any more selections. As she sat staring at the scarce leftovers, she watched everyone, man and dwarf, carry off their own dirty dishes to the kitchen. Two adorable dwarf girls came to help her with her plate. The children briefly quarreled with each other as to who would carry the glass and who would carry the utensils. In the end, Zandria carried all of her dishes and the girls were happy to trail behind, holding hands.

After the morning chores were finished, Professor Erbadin started organizing the work crews. He stopped long enough to instruct one of the soldiers to saddle Tihi for her.

"It's a shame that you won't stay longer," he said.

"I still want to travel to the West and South before going back to Castle Empyrean," she half-lied. She truly did want to see the other countries, but her mission was here now.

"Bah," snorted the dwarf. "This is the most beautiful of all the lands," he added with a smile. Then he gave another of his ground sweeping bows.

Zandria bowed back and then decided to hug the ancient dwarf. He hugged her back with surprisingly muscular arms. She was afraid he might have bruised one of her ribs in the process. She did not realize how strong dwarves were.

A few human women packed some food for Zandria. They waited by Tihi while the man finished checking the saddle straps. Zandria thanked them as graciously as possible and mounted the waiting Friesian. Tihi walked away from the castle gate and did not begin to canter until they were on the path leading east. Soon they were surrounded by trees heading to Truewood.

Now safely away from Castlewood Castle, Tihi asked, "How did you sleep?"

"It was wonderful," said Zandria. "I do wish I could have stayed longer. Still, there will be time for that later."

"Castlewood is a beautiful place, but when we cross into Truewood, you will discover the real majesty of the North."

Tihi kept them at a brisk pace and before they stopped for lunch, Zandria could tell they were in Truewood. The thick, brown trees with their lush foliage were replaced with tall, skinny, pale trees. There were wide spaces between them and their tops were adorned with thin, leafless branches. Except for a layer of mist scraping the ground, there was nothing on the forest floor besides rich, moist dirt. Although this forest stood open, Zandria felt more boxed in because of the mist than when she was surrounded by the massive trees of Greatwood. She also felt the majesty Tihi talked about. Something in the air caused her to feel the thousands of years of elven greatness.

A shiver passed down Zandria's neck. She said, "I feel like we're being watched."

"I expect so," answered the Friesian. "The elves guard their land diligently. They know who moves within their borders at all times."

Tihi must not have liked the echo of her gallop in this new emptiness. She slowed to a walk and Zandria pressed tightly to her neck.

"Do you know who we are looking for?" Tihi broke the silence.

"Well, no." said Zandria. "Tym said to go to his family. They would help me."

"Which is his clan?"

"I don't know. He never said," answered Zandria.

"Then I'll take you to mine," said Tihi. She began to gallop again, this time with purpose.

Zandria surmised that Tihi knew her course well. Once or twice, she did not even pause when she came to a fork in the road. Zandria wondered what Tihi meant by *her clan*. Knowing the horse's distrust of elves, she became confused.

Aloud, Zandria said, "I thought you didn't like elves."

"I said I don't trust them. I never said I didn't like them. I was raised by elves."

That seemed like a wonderful thing to Zandria. She only knew one elf and that was Tym. Still, she heard others talk about their mystery and magic that was even older than the power of the first queen.

As they galloped along, they were suddenly flanked by two blurring figures. Something was moving fast on either side of them and Zandria could not make out what it was. Zandria wondered if these fast-moving figures were elves.

She stared at the blur on her left and in an instant, everything seemed to move in slow motion. She discovered the figure next to her was an elf. He was tall, probably taller than Tym, and looked very strong. He was bald except for two thick strips of hair that ran down the back of his head. For some reason, she found herself curious as to whether he had to shave his head to keep it that way. He had nothing beneath him, but his own two bare feet. His sharp, pointed toenails dug into the dirt with each step and he effortlessly stayed slightly ahead of the horse. He had no horse or other creature of his own to keep up this amazing speed. Zandria could not believe it when he winked at her.

To her right, Zandria turned to see the other shape was that of a female elf. This one was beautiful with her sharp features. The length of the woman's hair impressed Zandria. It trailed behind her past the end of Tihi's tail. Zandria wondered how the elf could run, or even walk, without constantly tripping on the silky white trusses.

She, like the male elf, looked like a hunter. They were both dressed in animal skins and each had various knives strapped to their upper arms and thighs. Plus they both had powerful looking bows slung across their backs with a quiver of arrows in easy reach.

Then the moment passed and the two figures were blurs again. Zandria now knew the elves had great speed, but suspected that their hidden images were aided by some magic. She did not think they were so quick as to be almost completely hidden from sight. She thought if that were so, then they would be so far ahead that Tihi could not keep up with them.

The distraction of the two hunters caused Zandria to lose track of their path. She hoped it would not come to that, but she knew she could never find her way out of Truewood on her own now. The elven escorts stayed close until they eventually came upon a small camp.

There were six tents in a clearing surrounding a fire pit. Several elves were preparing an evening meal at the fireside. The two elves that had traveled with them moved and knelt before an extremely old looking woman. The woman looked so old that she could not even open her eyes. Her pointy ears were bent and shriveled with age. The runner with the striped head whispered to her in their native tongue and she nodded. Zandria could not understand any of what was said.

As soon as the old woman nodded, Zandria was snagged out of the saddle by two other elves. She struggled at first, thinking Tihi was right about not trusting elves. They carried her straight toward the fire. Zandria did not think elves were cannibals, but she was afraid they were going to throw her into the fire. They stopped at the edge and sat her down on a mat made from the softest leaves she had ever felt. The female hunter with the long hair handed her a bowl of soup. Still shaken by the thought of being eaten, Zandria slowly sipped at the hot liquid.

While she ate, a young girl came out of the farthest tent. Zandria guessed she and this elf had to be about the same age. Zandria studied the girl as she came closer. She was dressed all in black, including a tunic and tight fitting pants. Her boots came up to her knees and were equally as black as the single, thick braid of hair that hung over her shoulder. Zandria expected her to have black eyes as well, but they were quite silver. When the elf sat next to her, Zandria saw age in her eyes. She knew this girl was not ten or twelve years old and suddenly understood that elves lived much longer, slower lives.

"They do not speak your language," said the girl. "I am sorry."

Zandria did not know how to respond, so she did not answer.

"Do you understand me? The others speak only Elvish. You can talk to me," continued the girl.

Zandria looked back at Tihi who was drinking from a bucket while being unsaddled.

Tihi must have caught the look and said, "It's okay. This is Dew Lantisphere. She raised me until I left for Castlewood."

"Can I trust her?" asked Zandria.

"She is the only elf I trust," said Tihi.

Zandria turned back to Dew Lantisphere and said, "I am so sorry. This is quite an unusual place for me. You can understand that I'm a little nervous."

"More than a little," said Dew. "Relax. I'm only forty-four. I'm a child like you."

The idea of a forty-four year old person being thought of as a child put a smile on Zandria's face. She instantly felt at ease. Tym sent her here for a reason, so she decided to tell Dew everything. She started by introducing herself and briefly summarizing her and Olena's journey to Castle Empyrean. She showed the crystal to Dew and explained that Tym told her to search Blackwood Forest.

"First of all, I would not trust anything that Tym says," said Dew.

"What?" said Zandria.

"I'm kidding. I know how Tihi is about elves. She's probably been filling your head with all kinds of stories. Tym's okay. His mother went to serve at the castle back when our people had better relations with humans. He's never set foot in Truewood, but he was right in sending you to us."

"You're his clan?" asked Zandria in surprise. She wondered to herself about the remote possibility of Tihi being raised by somebody from Tym's clan. The coincidence was too amazing for her.

"Some of us still consider him family," said Dew. Then she glanced at the ancient woman, "But some of us do not consider him at all."

"He said you can help me. Can you?" begged Zandria.

"I've never heard of this crystal and I've been close to Blackwood more times than I would like," said Dew. "I haven't been since before Tihi could chew a bit though, so I'm game."

Thrilled with Dew's answer, Zandria could not wait to start the next part of her trip.

Then Dew continued, "Still, it is an ill-advised course. Oh, and we may have to fight our way through the mines."

"Fight? What mines?" Zandria's confidence started waning.

Tihi nudged Dew from behind. She said to Zandria, "She's teasing you. We'll be fine."

Dew laughed, then hugged Zandria tightly. She said, "Tomorrow is yet to be seen. Tonight let us listen to the stories of the elders and dream of a glorious passage into the twilight."

The thought of passing into anywhere did not make Zandria feel better. Soon, she was distracted by the musical sound of the Elvish tongue.

The surviving members of the Lantisphere Clan told stories around the fire long into the night. Zandria had no idea what they were saying, but it mesmerized her. She ate and drank the food and drink as they passed it around, without looking at what she put in her mouth. Her eyes stuck to each member of the family as they took turns standing over the fire. This kept Zandria riveted. The story from the longhaired huntress caused it's teller to weep. Zandria did not understand a word, but she cried too.

The liquid in the leather flask she drank from caused her head to swim. Zandria felt it more when one of Dew's uncles jumped up shouting. His tale must have been full of danger and adventure, she thought, by the way he swung his wide curved sword as he spoke. The warrior seemed surreal and frightening at the same time through the haze of the strong elven drink.

This night, Zandria did not dream of the future, but of their striking narrow faces illuminated from below, casting shadows over their eyes. In her dream, she could only see the flames reflecting off their pointed teeth.

As Zandria fell asleep, the last thing she remembered was the old woman, who must have been Dew's grandmother, opening her eyes. She looked straight at Zandria with her milky, blind eyeballs and spoke in her own language. Somehow, even though this was the same tongue in which the others were telling their stories, the elder's words had no lyrical quality to them. The message felt like a warning meant for her. Zandria was not sure if this was dream or reality as she drifted away from the waking world.

Zandria let her own eyes fall closed and did not hear Dew respond to her grandmother. Dew replied in her elven language with something that roughly meant, "Her life is my responsibility as I take up this task. Death will have to beg me for an audience with her."

Chapter 8

The Trip to Bond

Too much knowledge meant too much pain.
Prince William had too much of both as
Squire to the Queen of the Eastern Sky. He
remembered when he took that title, it made him
proud. Of course, he thought, that was five
hundred years ago.

Today, he stood in the courtyard of the Palace
by the Sea. He knew other eyes saw the sand and
glass of the palace, but he saw only her, the one
who built it. His love for her brought him to this
moment.

William knew when she became Queen of the
Eastern Sky, they would never be married. Still, he
swore to wait for her when she left for the new
land by the sea. That is when she built this palace.
That is when he remained to grow old.

He realized now that being one of the four
queens is a great responsibility. It is something far

bigger than the love or even life of one person. He always hoped that she did not forget him. However, he doubted that because she never sent for him either.

There was one moment, when he had a thought, a sudden and pure thought, that he should go to her.

By that time, it was already too late. He already lost that part of himself that aspired for something more. He spent his days by the fountain in the garden. He knelt, sometimes praying, sometimes waiting. She never sent for him and, without hope, his heart grew cold. He did not feel himself freeze. He did not see the abandoned village of Fountainhead crumble around him. He did not know as five hundred years passed.

Then two young girls, two sisters, awoke him from his dream. At least, it felt like a dream because it definitely did not feel real. At that moment, his life changed again. When they took his love away to be queen, he still had a chance to be with her. Now, so many years later, he found her taken away again. This time he had no chance.

He swore allegiance to the girl who would be queen. At that moment, he knew that was enough.

In his heart, William still felt young, as young as he was on the day she left. His body betrayed him, however. When he first awoke from his five hundred year slumber, he could barely move. As he found a purpose and a new direction, he regained his physical self as well.

On that last ride across the plains, William had become the man he once was. He told Fury that he felt complete. As the dragon Evorin flew over his head and into battle with the Rockhorn army, he even felt younger and stronger.

Then he came here. He knew he had to help Adam and the children imprisoned in the mine.

Unfortunately, five hundred years did not prepare him for his feelings when he saw her in every detail of the magnificent Palace by the Sea. He knew she was gone. He knew her castle Soria Moria laid in ruins. He did not know her love and energy still held this place together.

Feeling her again after so long wrenched his heart. He lost her twice. This knowledge triggered something in him. He noticed it first when his clothes stopped fitting correctly. His body started changing again. He hoped it would be a momentary thing. He hoped it would stop.

Having his pants fall down did not embarrass him, but he knew it showed everyone else what was happening. Adam saw it first. William liked Adam because he reminded him of himself. Adam was smart. He noticed things.

The others seemed to accept it, or at least not question it. The northerner, Terg, made a joke about it. Otherwise, they seemed to trust him and follow his lead.

Now, he led them past the seaside village of Banookanook. He looked at the huts made of wood and giant seashells. He thought, this is where my new queen called home. He liked Olena. He swore to protect her, but Olena would never replace *her*.

The Nookans watched the travelers from the safety of their huts and boats. It appeared that life already started returning to normal at this edge of Empyrean. William found some comfort in the thought of a normal world, but he knew this was not his world. He wanted it to be, but did not know how that could ever be possible.

William looked back at his party, straggling the length of the pristine Nookan beach. Sulis seemed happy to be the lead horse, but the other Friesians looked battle weary.

The young-looking Smoltz Brothers darted around on foot, trying to keep the emancipated children in a single line. They could have been triplets, except William knew a year or two separated each.

Humboldt and Reinholdt, still dressed in their war-torn royal finery shared a mount. They both seemed so out of place. William wondered what the two young men thought of the world beyond the West. He recalled their land was one of peace and tradition. Royal masquerades and elegant gardens must have been their primary concern until very recently.

William then watched Aleta issuing firm instructions from atop another Friesian. She looked uncomfortable, probably because she was used to standing in the harness of a giant crocodile instead of a horse. Aside from her obvious discomfort, he noticed her beauty for the first time. Her dark features were so different from the women of his land, even those of the Nookans. While the beach-dwelling Nookans were dark skinned, Aleta seemed to have absorbed the golden shine of the sun as well.

The last Friesian followed the group, carrying Terg who stared at the ocean like he had never seen it before. His rough features were subdued by the innocent awe brought on by the repetitive waves. William knew Terg was not an old man, but the recent battles made him look haggard and etched worried wrinkles across his unshaven face.

The strong-willed soldier looked ready to kick off his boots and splash in the waves. William knew his gradual unaging could become a problem with Terg. Already, the soldier did not hesitate to challenge him. If he did not stop getting younger soon, Terg might start treating him like one of their refugees. For now, William hoped he would be distracted by the new scenery.

As Adam said, Prince William found the opening in the dense jungle wall. He guided Sulis toward it and they left the beach behind.

The thick jungle made the going slow. The twisting branches and wide, rubbery leaves forced everyone to the ground. The horses could not navigate through the growth carrying anyone on their backs. It disappointed William that they had to spend the night here before they reached the wasteland or even the Great Cliffs.

With the start of the next morning, William discovered a change in the landscape. The remnants of the Royal Forest mixed in with the coastal jungle. This unusual combination actually made their travel easier. The trees grew further apart like they could not decide which one should have the space, so neither palm nor broadleaf took it.

He had no way of knowing, but before lunch, they entered the same creek bed that Zandria and Olena walked in not so long ago. The ground here dipped from hundreds, if not thousands, of years of the little creek cutting its way through the forest to the mighty river. William felt relieved to be at the Chromisarc River. He remembered the name from the map he sent with Adam. He also remembered it marked the halfway point on the trip to Bond.

From here, they had to turn south against the flow of the river. It took Terg and the Smoltz Brothers a while to find an area safe enough to take the children across. This took most of the afternoon, as the adults had to carry most of the children across the fast-moving, knee-deep water. Aleta and the Northern men carried two at a time, while William, Hum and Reinholdt could only manage one child and keep their balance.

This lack of strength frustrated William. He knew his body was fit and strong for its age, however, that age was now less than he was used to. Yesterday, he could have carried two children and one on his back, he chided himself. This growing younger did not only affect him, he thought, but also the safety of those he was charged to protect.

After the exhausting crossing, William decided to let his party rest. They made an impromptu camp on the west bank of the Chromisarc. As he drifted in and out of a nap, he imagined movement on the opposite bank of the river. When the water splashed right in front of him, he realized it was not his imagination.

Three dwarves had slowly and quietly crossed the river. Now they were on him. William had no time to draw his sword and had to wrestle them by hand.

"Terg, I could use some help over here," he shouted. His voice cracked, reminding him again of his body's betrayal. If it had been only a day earlier, he would have had no problem fighting three dwarves. He lied to himself that he could defeat five of them.

Terg responded quickly, shaking off his sleep like a well-trained soldier. As quickly as he could, he dispatched one of the dwarves. The second did not see the flash of his sword before it struck. Then the third dwarf disappeared into the tree line. A moment later, the same dwarf burst out of the undergrowth with a fierce battle cry, swinging his axe. The oldest of the young Smoltz Brothers did not react in time. His limp body fell face first into the mud at the river's edge. Then the dwarf vanished again.

"Vanril," Terg screamed.

William could see rage and hatred in the Northern soldier's eyes. Terg started to run after the dwarf and William grabbed his arm. His smaller body was no match for Terg's broad shouldered mass. The enraged soldier dragged him along.

"You must stop this," demanded William. "We have to protect the children. There could be more of them."

Terg stopped. He turned, grabbed William by the front of his shirt and lifted him off the ground.

He said, "I don't care if there are a hundred more. Vanril is mine. It is not enough that he poisons my homeland. Now he attacks sleeping children like a coward."

"You can't do this," said William.

"I don't have a choice. That is my countryman lying there." He pointed at the eldest Smoltz with his free hand.

"And it is their brother," said William, gesturing to the remaining Smoltz Brothers. One stood in tears while the other seethed, squeezing his sword hilt so tight that his knuckles turned white.

Terg looked at the other two men. He let go and William dropped down on his backside. Terg strode to the Smoltz Brothers and hugged them, one in each arm. The three men cried silently. William thought it looked like a father and his sons. The late afternoon sun made Terg's hair look a little more gray. Also, he knew the Smoltz' were young, but their faces now looked like nothing more than lost teenagers. Still, they were probably older than he was at this point.

Aleta helped William to his feet and he said, "We will find Vanril. I promise." The three men turned to him. William continued, "First, we have to get these young ones to safety. For whatever reason, that dwarf intends to do harm to them. It is likely he will strike again. It is also likely that there are more dwarves with him."

"Fine," said Terg. "I'll go with you as far as Bond. I will do my duty to see these children to their families. But these two are going to avenge their brother. I'll work triple so that they can search for Vanril. He followed us from the Palace by the Sea and attacked us at our weakest. I won't allow that to happen again."

William considered how they would manage so many children with three less caretakers. He never had a brother, but knew what it was like to lose someone. He decided to let them go for that reason and because he believed Terg was an honorable man. If Terg could handle the children as he said, then they could make it without the surviving Smoltz Brothers.

"You have my word," said William. "When we leave Bond, I will help you put a stop to Vanril for once and good."

He offered his hand and Terg shook it with his own dry, tough hand. William could feel the difference in strength as their difference in age increased. He thought he must not look more than a teenage boy to this hard, middle-aged man.

Before they continued their journey, they buried the eldest Smoltz on the bank of the Chromisarc River. The western gardener, Reinholdt, carefully arranged some flowers that he found in the surrounding forest.

He said, "These at the head will bloom every year to mark this spot."

"An inadequate tribute for such a sacrifice, but it is appreciated," said Terg.

While Hum, Reinholdt and Aleta rounded up their wards, Terg gave instructions to the Smoltz Brothers. William did not hear what was said, but he saw it said with conviction. Right now, he happily accepted the problem of his coming youth over ever wanting to be Vanril, or any dwarf that happened to be on the pointed end of a Smoltzsword.

Surprisingly, William found their party did not move much slower. Terg stayed on foot, allowing his Friesian to corral the children from one side while he stayed on the other. They kept the kids together and constantly moving like that for the rest of the day.

Before dark, they crossed into the wasteland. They were so far south, that always to their left, William could see the Dead Forest, where the wasteland had not eaten away at it. Beyond that were the unknown lands of the far South that did not show on any Eastern map. Even in his time, he never knew anyone who ventured that way to return.

The wasteland did not slow them much either because they moved along its southern edge. Here, they avoided the worst of the cracks and sinkholes. Terg pressed everyone on long after dark, but William insisted they stop.

"I think we will have to spend another night out here," he said. "For the children's sake, I hope we do not have to sleep in the Dead Forest."

"Isn't their town in the Dead Forest?" asked Terg.

"I think some magic still protects that last of the towns. Bremen was like an oasis, maybe Bond will be too," said William.

"I will stand watch tonight," offered Aleta.

Terg said, "That is my task."

"The time will come for you to be a hero," said Aleta. "Now is not it. Reserve some strength for the moment when you need it."

This warrior woman from the South impressed William. Apparently, she had some effect on Terg as well. He found a spot to sleep without another word. William fell asleep, watching the tall, strong woman standing over the children, holding her spear. He knew she did not have to be a queen to be powerful.

They finished crossing the wasteland the next day. Soon the Dead Forest bordered them on the side and in front in the distance. The entire day passed without a sign from the Smoltz Brothers. William hoped that they had seen the last of Vanril. Then, he thought, what if Vanril finished off the Smoltz family? He feared Terg would be uncontrollable then. This was not something he wanted to experience.

To his relief, the brothers caught up with them at the edge of the Dead Forest. They reported finding some tracks, but nothing more. They did not think Vanril crossed the wasteland alone, but they could not identify the other tracks they found. The only thing they knew for sure was that the footprints were much larger than a dwarf.

William suggested they spend the night at the edge of the wasteland before they got into any worse part of the Dead Forest. When he awoke in the morning, the Smoltz Brothers were already back to their hunt. Terg and Aleta prepared the children for another day of walking while Hum and Reinholdt made breakfast for everyone.

When Hum brought William some food, he said, "Do you realize how much you look like that other fellow?"

William could feel his body smaller today, but did not know who Hum referred to. "Which one?" he asked with amused curiosity.

"The boy, Adam," Hum said.

This shocked William. He never thought they might look alike. He must be younger than he realized at this point. He thought, maybe Hum thinks they look alike because they are both now about the same age. There could not be any similarity other than a Westerner observing two Easterners. He laughed at the suggestion and thought nothing else about it.

They were closer to Bond than William realized. They only had to walk for a few hours that morning. A short way into the forest, they found an abandoned road. The dirt road led them straight to Bond. When they first walked into the town with its odd shaped buildings, William thought the place looked deserted. He noticed the children did not act like they recognized it either.

He worried now that they came all this way for nothing. If he had known that before coming, he would have saved everyone the pain.

Chapter 9

A Meeting at the Mines

She could barely remember anything of the previous night when she woke. Zandria felt dazed and very alone in the middle of this spooky forest. There was no sign of the elves, their camp or even the fire that kept her warm most of the night. All she saw was mist drifting between the skinny, pale trees. She sat up in a panic because she did not even see Tihi at first. To her relief, the Friesian stood only a short distance away, eating some of the grass that proved to be rare in Truewood.

Zandria did not think she dreamt the elves. However, as she concentrated on it more, she allowed the possibility that it was all in her imagination. First, there was the pair of blurry, fast-moving elves. Then their camp appeared out of nowhere and it quickly became dark immediately after that. The thing that caused her to doubt herself the most was that they spoke in a strange language. If it were a dream, she thought, why would she only be able to understand one of them. All of them spoke that way except for one.

She tried to remember that girl's name, something to do with water.

"Hi," said Dew from behind her. Zandria spun around to see Dew Lantisphere dressed in the same black clothes from last night. She thought the elven girl looked quite like a thief. Then she remembered that Dew was not a girl. Despite how the elf appeared, Zandria believed her statement of being forty-four years old. This thought made her wonder how old Dew's blind grandmother might be, because she looked really old to Zandria. Now, Zandria started doubting her doubts. The mysterious elves must have been real, she realized.

Tihi came over when Dew appeared. She said, "Good morning, you two."

Dew rubbed a hand on Tihi's neck behind her jaw. Zandria could see the love shared between them. She remembered Tihi saying that Dew raised her. Then Dew slipped her other hand into a hidden pocket and pulled out a long, yellow vegetable. At least, Zandria guessed it to be a vegetable by the way Tihi quickly ate it.

"I haven't been in these woods since I was a foal," Tihi said after chewing.

"It has been too long, has it not?" asked Dew.

Zandria liked seeing old friends rejoined, but she did not want to be left out of the conversation either. She asked, "So you two know each other?"

Dew turned her sharp, silver eyes to Zandria. The intensity Zandria saw there made her slightly uncomfortable. Dew explained, "The Friesian brigade is supposed to be only for the best stallions. When a female is born, they are usually turned loose into the woods. It isn't until they're much older that mares are brought back to Castlewood for labor. I found Tihi wandering lost about twenty years ago. My cousin and I trained her to be a warrior in the tradition of our clan. When the time was right, she went back to them with our secret silence."

The elf trailed off into her own silence, but Zandria guessed the rest. Apparently, Tihi's training and dedication earned her a trusted place among the Friesians, even though she pretended to be mute. Fury seemed to think highly of her in any case.

"Now, where did you want to go?" asked Dew with a smile that briefly showed her pointed teeth.

"Well, Tym said," started Zandria.

"Enough of the *Tym said*," interrupted Dew. "We are all women here. Can we please forget about men and their inadequacies for now? Where is it that *you* want to go?"

Zandria felt a contagious jolt of confidence from Dew. The elf made her realize that she could be strong on her own. She liked the males in her life, but Adam, William and even Fury were not here now. This task was given to her by her mother and she could finish it without a *man's* help. Zandria straightened up when she spoke, "*I* believe the next crystal is in Blackwood Forest."

"Then, as you know, we have to pass through the Dire Mines," said Dew.

"I remember Professor Erbadin talking about them," said Zandria.

"The Dire Mines are where the dwarves first came above ground. Until they swore an oath to the first queen, all they did was dig tunnels without the joy of the sun. After Vanril's faction revolted..."

Zandria interrupted, "I know about Lord Vanril. He attacked Castle Empyrean."

"Was he killed?" asked Dew.

"No."

"Then it probably won't be the last time. Now, as I was saying, since Vanril's three families left about a hundred years ago, the mines have been deserted. Nobody goes there, probably because they are haunted now," finished Dew.

"Haunted?" Zandria did not like the sound of that.

"No, I'm kidding. I like to tease, if you didn't notice," said Dew. "We might run into a few curses hiding in there, but nothing we can't handle."

"What do you mean curses?"

Tihi took her turn to explain, "Before curses are spoken in words, they exist as small creatures that usually hide in the forests. They are mischievous, but not normally dangerous unless spoken aloud."

Zandria thought they sounded like they might be unfriendly versions of quzzaks. She knew Kez and his family always used to be mischievous, especially when food was involved. With the strength she felt from both Dew and Tihi, she was not worried though.

Dew mounted Tihi first, which left Zandria to sit on the back of the saddle. She was not sure how this made her feel. She knew Tihi and Dew were old friends, but she wanted to be in front. It did not seem right for her to be in back when she had been with Tihi all this time. She quickly decided she was being trivial and it did not matter who was in front, as long as they got there together.

They headed into the forest, but Zandria could not tell which way they were going. She guessed it had to be north because that was the direction of Blackwood. Still, she saw no path or any indication of a route. As far as she could tell, the forest looked the same in all directions. She thought she might become depressed by the lifelessness, if the forest did not leave her feeling so uneasy.

Zandria wondered how such an empty place got a name like Truewood. Speaking barely above a whisper to avoid the echo of her own voice, she asked Dew about it.

"It doesn't have anything to do with the wood," said Dew.

"Go on, dear," interjected Tihi, "I appreciate the irony every time I hear it."

Dew made a face like she was offended and then smiled. "It's not true," she said.

"The story's not true?" asked Zandria. She felt left out of the joke.

"No," explained Dew. "The story is true. Tihi's firm belief that we are all liars is not true. We elves had no use or arrogance for naming the trees. When the first humans settled here, they felt they had to name everything. My ancestors welcomed them and our forest was so named because they believed we only spoke the truth."

"But Tihi doesn't," Zandria tried to joke.

Dew twisted around in the saddle. Zandria pulled back from the anger she saw in Dew's eyes.

"I'm sorry...I didn't..." stumbled Zandria.

Then Dew laughed and the upset look disappeared. The elf said, "Of course we only speak the truth. It depends on your perspective as to how you interpret it."

Zandria felt confused. This elven woman, who looked like a girl, seemed mad one moment and happy the next. She did not know what to make of her jokes that stung like fairy bites. Dew Lantisphere seemed strange. Yet, Zandria considered, maybe she was not strange for an elf.

As they passed through Truewood, Zandria told her own tale again. Dew appeared to listen intently, but she did not turn around once or even ask any questions.

When Zandria finished her story, Dew asked, "Did you ever think you might become queen?"

Her first response was to lie, but Zandria suspected Dew might be able to tell. Before she answered, a jumble of emotions rushed through her heart. She remembered feeling angry and alone. She had decided that she would be queen from the moment her father spoke of the possibility. She also remembered it feeling more like a burden than a gift and never once considered Olena as the fourth queen.

Zandria closed her eyes and felt the warmth that came to her back in the bell chamber of Empyrean. She only said, "I hoped."

Apparently, that answer was good enough for Dew because they did not talk anymore about it. Instead, they talked a little about Tihi's part in the Rockhorn Battle and how the dragon Evorin accidentally singed her tail during the fight. Then Dew suddenly seemed somber.

She said, "I love it when it snows in Truewood."

"What's snow?" asked Zandria. Apparently, Dew changed the topic of conversation as quickly and thoughtlessly as she changed moods. Zandria really did not know how to interpret her.

"It's what happens to rain when it gets too cold," said Dew. Then she added, "Where have you been your whole life?"

"On the beach," Zandria answered.

"Well, it only happens once every three or four years. But when it does, it gets so quiet. More than usual. You can't even hear your own breathing." Dew seemed excited by the nostalgia drifting in her own head. This made Zandria think of the frozen fountain where she found Prince William. If that was what snow was like, then she never cared if it got that cold again.

Before the sun sat in the east, they left Truewood for a wide field. Now that Zandria could see the sun again, she had her bearings back. Directly north of them was a sheer rock wall that ran off in either direction as far as she could see. At the base of the wall were continuous piles of rubble taller than Tihi. Zandria guessed the rock had fallen off the wall over the course of many years.

Dew jumped down from the saddle. "Blackwood is on the other side of that," she said, pointing to the wall. "I know the cliff is not that high, but it's too slippery and too sharp to climb."

Zandria studied the wall. She saw the razor edges where hundreds of years of rock gradually broke loose. She saw the height of the wall and guessed it was taller than any palm tree she had ever climbed back home. Even without Dew's warning, she would not want to attempt scaling a wall that flat. A fall from that distance might not killer her, but the piles of shattered rocks waiting below easily tripled that chance.

"Now we have to find a way inside," continued Dew.

"Inside?" asked Zandria. "Is this the mine?"

Tihi waited for Zandria to slide down from her back, then said, "Welcome to the Dire Mines."

Zandria moved as close to the wall as she could without mounting the rubble. She saw no sign of an entrance. "How do we get inside?" she asked.

"They're dwarves," quipped Dew, "Look on the ground."

As Dew said, a few paces away, Zandria found a hole that sloped steeply into the ground. She saw immediately that Tihi would not fit. Then, from further away, Dew shouted, "Over here."

Relieved to see this tunnel was much larger, Zandria noticed it was equally as steep and dark as the first. Before they started down, a noise came from inside the wide hole. It sounded to Zandria like breathing. She thought whatever was making that sound must be sick because the breathing was loud and scratchy.

After a moment of waiting, a creature emerged, walking on four short legs. Zandria's first impression was that it might be a baby horse because it only stood as tall as her waist. She did not think this was quite right because it had a lot of wooly brown hair. Then she noticed the thick, curved horns sticking out the two sides of its head and knew it was not a horse. Regardless of what it was, Zandria could tell the creature was in pain.

"It's a ram," said Tihi.

"It's a dwarf," retorted Dew.

Tihi said, "Don't be silly. Rams and sheep herd through here all the time. Dwarves even used them to pull their mine carts. This one must have been lost or left behind."

Dew looked to be scolding Tihi, "That's fine, but this is a dwarf. He's been cursed."

Then the ram moved toward Zandria and collapsed at her feet. Dew quickly grabbed a small bottle from one of Tihi's saddlebags. She knelt next to the ram and checked to see if it was still breathing. Then she pried open its upward facing eyelid with the thumb and forefinger of her left hand. She held the tiny bottle in her right hand and popped off the stopper with her thumb. The elf tipped the bottle slightly so that only a single drop of the clear liquid fell into the ram's open, but unfocused eye.

"Now we see if we're too late," said Dew. She found her cork on the ground, plugged the bottle and went to put it back in the bag.

Zandria tried not to look away from the ram. She wondered what they might be too late for. The ram's breathing slowed. Suddenly, its whole body shivered. With the shiver, all of its hair fell off in a big clump, revealing a small dwarf underneath the wooly mess. Everything about him instantly changed from ram to dwarf, except the horns remained and his left hand still looked like a hoof.

He remained unconscious.

"That's what happens when we're too late," said Dew.

"What?" asked Zandria.

"If you are cursed too long, you never change back," explained Tihi.

"Or you die," added Dew.

The dwarf stirred from his sleep. Looking at his former left hand, he said, "Zat figures. Ran into a whole nest of curses down zere. One ov zem must haf got me."

"Did you name them?" asked Zandria. She noticed this dwarf's strange accent. She did not think he came from Professor Erbadin's family or any other dwarf's she had met.

"Zat's zee veird bit. Zey attacked me," he said.

Zandria looked to Dew, not sure what to believe. Dew seemed to accept his story, but this did not make Zandria feel better. She did not want to be down in a dark mine only to be attacked by little creatures.

"What's your name, dwarf?" asked Dew, helping him up by his good arm.

"Saman."

"Do you have anything else you're supposed to tell us?" said Dew.

Saman looked surprised by this question. Zandria thought it was odd as well.

"Zere's a camp on zee odder side," said the dwarf. "I can lead you srough zee mines."

"Avoiding the nest of curses, of course," added Dew.

"Ov course," said Saman.

Zandria tried to ask Dew how she knew that he was instructed to tell them anything, but the elf and dwarf were already heading underground. Tihi followed without a word. Zandria did not like the look of the dwarf. He was much dirtier and darker than those back at Castlewood Castle. He seemed sick and his voice was horse, but Zandria guessed that could be because he had been cursed. Still, something did not feel right about him or about Dew following with no real explanation. Zandria trusted the elf, so far, and knew they had to get through the mines anyway. Not wanting to be left alone, she dashed into the mine after them.

Chapter 10

The Trip to Soria Moria

Bond looked like an interesting town. At least, William thought so.

As he walked down the wide street, he saw the houses and buildings crammed together like they had been stacked on top of each other. Some had the rustic look of Bremen and a few even had shells like he had seen in Banookanook. There was no one overall style. Every house looked like it came from somewhere else.

Then William saw one building with a thatched roof and straight, upright timbers. It reminded him of his own home in Fountainhead. It did not feel like it had been that long, but this building seemed to come to him out of the past. He knew it was not magic. This building was built here, but it was built in the unique style of his village that had been gone for several hundred years.

William began to understand. Bond came into existence after he was frozen. Some of the buildings looked old, maybe a hundred years. Others looked almost brand new. Some looked ready to fall on their sides, carelessly slapped together. Yet, others looked meticulous and pristine.

He guessed someone created Bond as the Royal Forest started to die. That would explain the odd combination of styles. William suspected that people fled their homes all across the forest as the dwarves mined under them and stole their children. They must have brought what was left of their lives here. Bond became a melding of all the people of the East.

This made William proud that people could come together like this. Especially, when they faced such troubles. The Dead Forest and the wasteland claimed their lands and the wicked dwarves claimed their children. It made him sad that this new town did not survive to see the return of their children.

The party walked on through the empty town. The children marveled at store windows full of foods, clothes and, of course, toys. William could not understand how this deserted place could have such recently stocked wares.

As they turned corner after corner, William began to realize Bond was much larger than he anticipated. It made sense that Bond would be huge to accommodate frightened people from all across the East. Still, he did not imagine it to be this expansive.

"This place is bigger than Lochnoble," said Terg.

"Where is Lochnoble?" asked Hum.

"Lochnoble is home to the men of the North. It is my home and I miss it dearly."

William said, "I hope it is not as empty as this place."

Then Aleta tapped him on the shoulder. They had turned onto the widest street yet and at the end stood an enormous building. William guessed they were almost in the very center of Bond.

"I do not think we are so alone," said Aleta.

Bells on the four corners of the giant building started ringing. Then three sets of wide doors opened, spilling hundreds of people out into the late morning. They were laughing and gossiping. William thought he could hear singing coming from inside.

"Must be some kind of church," suggested Terg.

At the sound of his voice, the citizens of Bond froze, silent. Every eye focused on the strangers at the far end of the street. Under their gaze, William felt the distance between them stretch a mile. William had never felt this uncomfortable, as if they were disturbing something quite important.

Someone in the back of the childless crowd coughed, but otherwise it stayed silent. William knew the quiet did not last as long as it seemed. Then a woman collapsed, wailing. More sounds of crying broke out amongst the Bondsfolk. Cheers and hoorays followed this. Suddenly, the men and women were rushing towards them. The people swarmed William's small party, scooping children up into big hugs and shaking the hands of William and his friends.

His trepidation quickly vanished as William realized how grateful these people were to see their children. He guessed correctly that these people came from all parts of his homeland. Around him, parents looked on children they thought they would never see again. This feeling of reunion overwhelmed him.

Then he saw couples, some older, whose children never made it out of the mines. There was so much joy around him that he almost could not imagine the feelings of the lost ones. This made him think about her, his queen. He believed the loss of a bride could not compare to the loss of a child, but he told himself it was close.

An official looking man, official looking except that he had a long braid of gray hair running down his back that may never have been cut, started toward William, then turned to Terg.

Over his pleasant potbelly, he said, "I am Rud, Governor of Bond. I wanted to thank you for giving us a day we never dared imagine would come."

"Don't thank me," said Terg, "He's the one that saved them." Terg pointed at William.

"Forgive me," said Governor Rud. He started shaking William's hand violently. "I assumed you were one of the lost children. How is it someone so young came to do something so great?"

"I was older then," said William with a smile.

This brought a look of confusion to the governor's face. Then the crowd swept William and the others off to a large banquet hall.

Inside, the people of Bond celebrated to an excess rivaled only by the apparent love for their children. William could barely move after he stuffed himself full of food and drink.

William asked Governor Rud sitting next to him, "We thought this town was deserted?"

"Oh no. Every third day, we gather together to pray for the return of our children. Today, you answered our prayer."

"It was something I could not have done alone," William said, modestly. "I hope those that gave their lives bringing us here can receive this much praise."

"Without a doubt," said the governor. "I will dedicate this day to their memory. It is the smallest of gestures that we can do to have an annual festival celebrating the lives that gave us back ours. We believed ourselves cursed since no one has had a child in the past year. Not since the last baby was stolen. Maybe that will change now, too."

William noticed Terg get up from the table.

"Excuse me, Governor." William made his way to Terg, before the man could make it outside. "Where are you going?" he asked.

Terg looked at him coldly. He said, "To find Vanril."

"Let your food settle," said William, putting a hand on the soldier's arm to usher him back inside.

"You promised to help." Terg snatched his arm away. A few Bondsfolk noticed the commotion, but turned back to their feasting.

"And I will. I am a man, or boy as the case may be, of my word. First, we must formulate a plan. You cannot rush off into a strange land. Especially one that your enemy knows too well," said William.

William could see Terg calming. The northerner took a deep breath and said, "It is easy to forget you are not a child. Your wise words are the only thing cooling my boiling blood. Vanril has been a threat to my people for too long. Seeing what he has done to this land only worsens the pain."

"I understand. It is my country too which he has set to ruin," said William. "Today, let us find comfort in knowing that we brought part of this land back to life."

Terg slapped William on the shoulder and they rejoined the party.

After the feast ended, close to sunset, William and his friends were invited to spend the night each with different families. As they made their way into the street, the Smoltz Brothers came around the corner. Relieved to see them still alive, William watched them go straight to Terg. He could not get through the crowd in time to hear their conversation, but the older man followed the brothers without hesitation.

William wanted to help Terg and the Smoltz Brothers. He had his own reasons for wanting to go after Vanril. The dwarf caused the disaster that his home had become. He hoped Vanril would somehow know how to restore it. He did not know how to convince him to do it, but he wanted to capture Vanril and at least try. He knew Terg only wanted revenge. He knew Terg had a strong will with much honor and nothing could stop his determination. William went to sleep that night thinking he had lost his only chance to save his land.

William hoped Terg and the Smoltz Brothers would be there the next morning, but they did not return. The Governor graciously offered them a breakfast buffet and an invitation to stay as long as they wanted.

"For you, no request is denied," he said to William.

"In that case, I would like to see your birth records." William had another promise to keep. He did not want to let down everyone.

Governor Rud looked confused by the request, but led William to the Bond Library. As he unlocked the records room, he asked, "What are you hoping to find?"

"Another boy escaped the mine. Now he is on a task in service of the Queen of the Eastern Sky. I promised him I would try to find his family," explained William.

"If he was born in the last ten years, he'll be in here," said the Governor.

"What about before that?" asked William.

"Before that, Bond was only another small village in the Royal Forest. Over the last ten years was when most of the towns died out. That's when Bond's population more than tripled. Any records before that were kept at the Palace by the Sea."

This news did not make William happy. He knew Adam was more than ten years old, probably eleven. The possibility that his information could be here seemed slight. Still, William spent hours searching for any mention of his young friend. He thought it was ironic to think of Adam in that way, since he now appeared younger than an eleven year old. Maybe it was the satisfaction of returning the children, but William did not feel as if he was deaging as fast today.

After hours of reading and finally ready to give up, he came across a book for a village called Frostwick. He did not recognize the name, but from the description, it sounded very near his home of Fountainhead. The book had a hundred years' worth of births, marriages and deaths. The last birth entry was of a boy named Adam.

When William showed it to the governor, Rud looked amazed. He said, "I can't believe you found such a treasure. I thought I knew our records well. It was providence that put that tome in your hands, my boy."

William wanted to remind him, "I'm not a boy," but instead, he said, "Do you know anyone from this Frostwick or where it was located?"

Governor Rud thought for a moment. He said, "As I recall, some tragedy befell that village. Some tragedy other than the Dead Forest, I mean. In any case, the last survivor I know passed on last year. I remember being quite fond of the dear old lady as well. This book must have been in her possessions."

This seemed like good news, but William felt he did not make any real progress. He asked, "Where is Frostwick?"

"Gone now," said Governor Rud. "However, there might be one way to find your answer."

The governor had William's attention. "What would that be?"

"It may not exist any longer, but my grandfather told me of a place. I don't expect the name Soria Moria to mean anything to you, but it is the castle where the queen lived before the Palace by the Sea. I can't imagine how you would ever find it."

"I've been there," said William. He saw that he shocked Governor Rud for the second time.

William thanked the Governor for his hospitality and the Governor thanked him repeatedly for freeing their children. Then William gathered his comrades.

"We owe this to Adam," he explained. "I swore to aid Terg and the brothers, but, right now, we have no idea where they are. We can be to Soria Moria in three days according to these updated maps. The Governor here insists that records were maintained at Soria Moria even after the queen moved."

Aleta nodded her understanding. This made William glad to have her and her weapon at his side. Something about her stirred some other forgotten feelings in him as well. Hum did not look as enthusiastic about the proposition.

He spoke for both him and Reinholdt, "We are not the adventuring sort. Already, I've experienced more fighting these past weeks than in my entire life. Reiny and I would like to stay here for a while and help with the children. After that, we are going to find the most direct route home."

"I understand," said William. He felt saddened to be losing a loyal friend, but this was truly not Hum or Reinholdt's quest. "I am sure our paths will cross again. Until that time, safe journey."

They made their farewells that afternoon at the border of Bond. Then William and Aleta started the trip to Soria Moria.

Without the children or extra traveling companions, William and Aleta made fast time. They traveled on the Mountain Byway, an old road that ran along the length of the Euphoric Mountains. Sulis carried William, but the prince kept forgetting the name of the Friesian that offered to carry Aleta. He feared this onset of absent-mindedness was a symptom of growing younger. Maybe, he thought, a child's mind is not as developed and cannot hold as much information. Or, maybe the weak memory was a side effect of whatever caused the aging problem to begin with, he entertained.

At the end of second day of travel, they arrived at the intersection of the Great Road. William knew to the west stood the Castle Empyrean and to the east was the town of Bremen. He hoped camping in such an exposed area would be safe, but they had no other choice. He did not want to be attacked by dwarves while they slept again.

Aleta did not speak very much as they traveled, so William spent a lot of time with his own thoughts. Mostly, he concentrated on Adam's town of Frostwick. He entertained the possibility of Frostwick and his home of Fountainhead being the same place. He thought that would be an amazing coincidence. Then he dismissed the possibility because his town decayed into the woods while he knelt by the fountain for which the village was named.

William also thought about Terg. He wondered what the soldier would think of him now. Never in his life had he failed to keep a promise. There was only one thing more important than his word to him, and she was gone forever. Hopefully, Terg would be satisfied with defeating Vanril on his own if he could find him, and forgive William for failing him.

In the morning, William guided Sulis off the Mountain Byway and into the Dead Forest. Aleta and the other Friesian followed close. It did not take long and then they stood in the open field in front of Soria Moria.

His mind still played tricks on him. William almost expected the castle to be standing in its resplendent, flawless beauty from five hundred years ago. Instead, he found the same crumbling tower that wrenched his heart the day the Kappa wanted to eat Olena. He found one thing different though. The big iron front door had been smashed off its hinges, apparently from the inside. Luckily, there were no other signs of trolls or even that tricky Kappa.

Chapter 11

Something Wicked

As they walked through the low ceilinged mine, Zandria tried to figure out Saman the dwarf. Too much seemed unusual about him. First, he did not talk like any other dwarf she had met. Secondly, he did not look like any other dwarf she had seen recently. He seemed burned from the inside, like the good parts of him had been hollowed out. Oddly, he was the only dwarf she had seen without a beard. She did not know if this meant anything other than his own personal preference. She also thought it was way too convenient for him to stumble out of the first hole they found. Could he have been looking specifically for them, she wondered?

Zandria tried to remember what Dew said. She thought she said, "Was there something you were supposed to tell us". Not sure what that meant, the only thing she could guess was that Dew believed someone gave Saman orders to find them. It scared Zandria to think who that someone might be. She worried that the dwarf might be working for whoever trapped her mother. Her only solace was the possibility that one of the queens might have sent him instead. Still, Dew seemed intuitive and this made Zandria feel like she missed some secret about Saman.

She could not concentrate on the Saman problem too long because she kept hearing noises coming from the dark side tunnels. Zandria knew at any moment, a nasty little curse would spring out of the darkness. She imagined it having sharp claws and countless gnashing teeth. She knew they were small and thought that would make it harder to protect herself as it squirmed toward her.

Her imagination did not stop there. It scared her to think how it might try to get in her body. Would it crawl in her mouth or tear through her skin? Then after whatever painful way it took her over, what would she become? She did not want to be an animal, but what if it was something worse, like being invisible or getting a disease? Zandria's mind reeled from the horrible possibilities.

Throughout the night, Zandria's mind bounced between thoughts of the suspicious dwarf and the frightening curses. She did not dare talk to Dew or Tihi about it in case Saman overheard. She knew it would either alert him or offend him and she did not want to do either right now.

When they emerged on the north side of the mine, Zandria felt relieved to see the morning sun rising. She did not realize they had walked all night underground. Still, Zandria did not feel tired. Considering everything else, she was quite happy to not have discovered what a curse really looked like.

The field they were now standing in did not look much different than the one they left last night, except there was no rock wall looming over them. When she looked back to the south, Zandria thought she could make out the edge that dropped off to where the lower ground entered the mine the night before. Seeing this new field dotted with sheep and the occasional ram strangely amused her. She wondered if these were real animals or more cursed dwarves.

The sight to the north turned her stomach though. From where they were standing, Zandria could pick up a rock, throw it and hit the closest tree in Blackwood Forest. She did not need Dew or Tihi to tell her where they were. These slimy trees were unmistakable. The oil glistened as it oozed out of the black bark. The long feathery black leaves brushed at the ground on thin sagging branches. When a breeze blew, the trees looked to Zandria like they were crying as the shiny leaves twirled.

"Now what?" said Dew.

Zandria thought the elf was talking to her, but Saman answered in his thick accent, "Now vee vait."

The Blackwood Forest already made her feel uneasy. Now Saman telling them to wait for something pushed her closer to dread. Zandria could not understand why Dew chose to trust this stranger. Zandria thought it was now obvious that the dwarf was sent by someone. She guessed Dew wanted to find out who it was.

They did not have to wait long for something to happen.

After an uncomfortable moment of silence, Zandria heard the faint rattling of chains and clanking like two pans banging together. In the distance, she saw something coming towards them along the tree line. At first, she thought it was the skinniest house she had ever seen. Then she saw it riding on four large, spindly wheels. As it got closer, Zandria feared the wheels might break under the weight because they looked too thin to hold up the narrow house.

Then she recognized the poor creature pulling the cart. This donkey did not look much different than the one she saw in Bremen, but she knew it was not the same one. This pathetic creature looked starved and the scars on his back made Zandria think the driver was too quick with the whip. She could not believe this sickly-looking donkey was able to pull this oversized wagon with its clanking cookware dangling from the sides.

Now, Zandria turned her attention to the driver sitting on the narrow bench high above the chained donkey. The tall, skinny man wore a tall, skinny hat. He had no mustache, but his shiny, black beard curled up and pointed the tip back toward his mouth. His tanned skin made it look like he was wearing makeup. The makeup effect extended to the black outlining his eyes, which trailed off into little points making him look quite sinister. She thought his all white suit with the ruffled chest and cuffs made him look evil. Then he curled his thin, black-stained lips into a smile that made Zandria feel even worse.

The disquieting driver pulled hard on the reins and snapped his whip, making Zandria wince. As the donkey gagged on the bit in his mouth, he braced himself for the weight of the wagon to slam against him before it stopped moving.

Once the wagon halted, the man stood up and with an exaggerated wave of his arm, said, "Allow me to introduce myself. I am Raymond Shaydaway, founder and curator of the Carnivale Chaotica and Pandemonium Sideshow."

"So, this is who we were waiting for," said Dew. She did not look impressed.

Saman moved next to the wagon. He craned his neck up at the man towering far above him. He said, "I brought zem, master. Zey vere right vere you zaid zey'd be. I got curzed on zee vay, but..."

"Enough," interrupted Shaydaway.

The dwarf fell silent instantly. Shaydaway seemed to relish his control.

Shaydaway continued, "Please, step around my humble cart and I will show you what we have to offer."

Zandria noticed the frightening man said *we*. She glanced around to see no one beside or behind him. There was no one anywhere on the field that stretched out behind the cart. She wondered briefly if there might be someone inside the wagon. She felt this would be a bumpy and uncomfortable way to ride from the look of the wobbly wheels.

Dew led the way around the wagon and Zandria followed close behind her. When she cleared the far side, she was stunned. Busy people now filled the field, setting up tents and small booths. Zandria could not believe what she was seeing. When Shaydaway rolled up to them, there was no one else around for miles. Now, suddenly, there were a dozen more tents and at least thirty people.

"Bad magic," Zandria mumbled, thinking to herself how much she sounded like Kez.

With a feeling at the back of her neck, Zandria spun around to find Shaydaway staring at them. He leaned far over the side of his wagon seat and she thought he looked menacing. As soon as they made eye contact, he quickly replaced his evil look with the creepy smile from earlier. The man did not yet do anything overtly threatening, but Zandria did not trust him.

"My associates will have everything ready soon," said Shaydaway. "While you wait, Saman will prepare you a meal."

When Shaydaway turned his back, Zandria looked to Dew. She tried to convey her worry with a quick expression. Dew shrugged her shoulders like she did not understand what Zandria wanted to tell her. Trying not to make a sound, Zandria pointed at the carnival and back at Shaydaway. She wanted Dew to understand she was scared, but she was too afraid to say it aloud.

Then Saman burst out of the back door of the wagon. The surprise appearance startled Zandria because she did not see him go in the cart. This sudden movement coupled with the polka-dotted apron the dwarf was now wearing forced a yelp from her.

Climbing down the narrow ladder from his high bench, Raymond Shaydaway said, "Don't be nervous milady. We are but simple entertainers. Nothing to be afraid of."

His words only made Zandria that much more concerned. Still, Dew did not look in the least worried. She climbed up into the wagon, so Zandria followed. Saman made a stew and Zandria ate quickly, but cautiously. She wanted to get out of the cramped space as soon as possible. Boxes, bags, musical instruments and camping supplies looked like they might topple on the passengers at any moment. As soon as she finished her one bowl, she politely excused herself.

When she stepped outside, her shock returned. Zandria saw, after only a few moments inside, that the mysterious crew had set up the entire carnival. They erected two rows of booths, interspersed with several small tents. Both rows ran parallel to each other and led to one giant tent at the far end of the aisle.

Darkness fell quickly and the eerie glow of paper lanterns strung from booth to booth beckoned her like a night crab to a beach fire back home. Zandria looked around and saw Tihi sharing a salt lick with the miserable donkey. The Friesian looked as much at ease as the elf around these strangers. Zandria could not believe that either of her traveling companions seemed bothered by their surroundings. In her apprehension, she decided to wait for Dew to finish eating before exploring the sideshow.

After what seemed like too long, Dew finally came out of the wagon. She wiped her mouth on her sleeve and grinned at Zandria like she might have enjoyed the salty broth.

"I don't like this place," whispered Zandria.

Dew whispered back, "Pretend like you do."

The elf continued to look at her with, what Zandria thought, an exaggerated smile. Then Zandria realized she was faking. Whatever was going on here, Zandria now understood that they must go along with it. Perhaps, she deduced, something bad would happen if they tried to ask too many questions or leave unexpectedly.

At the far end of the bazaar, Zandria saw the opening to the large tent ruffle. Saman appeared, pulling back the bright yellow flap to make a large opening. She knew it was Saman because she could see his ram's horns from where she stood, but she never saw him leave the wagon. This keeps getting weirder, she thought. Saman held the curtain so that Mister Raymond Shaydaway could make his entrance. The tall, skinny man gracefully and deliberately bowed to them. He did not say a word, but gestured that they make their way past the exhibits to join him at the far end.

"Come on. Let's play a game," Dew said as she headed for the first booth.

Zandria did not know if she actually meant one of the sideshow games or a mental game with Shaydaway. Glancing down the aisle, the games looked like fun. Most appeared to be games of skill such as throwing knives at targets. Still, she wondered if their game was to hide the purpose of their trip from Shaydaway. Maybe both, she decided as she joined Dew, who was throwing rather small balls at some rather large bottles, trying to knock them over.

This looked like fun to Zandria and for an instant, she forgot her fear. Then she looked at the person tending the booth. At least, she thought it was a person. The attendant dressed in bright colors like the other workers she saw from a distance. This one had a red, long-sleeve shirt under a blue vest. Zandria could not tell if it was a human because the face was blurry. It looked, to her, like the head was moving unbelievably fast, bouncing from side to side and sometimes spinning around all the way. Randomly, the face stopped for an instant, but all Zandria could make out was a look of sheer terror.

"What's wrong with that person?"

"It's an interloper," Dew said, concentrating on her aim.

"What does that mean?" Zandria did not like the sound of it.

"It's somebody that tried to crossover from another dimension without the correct knowledge of how to do it. Now they're trapped," said Dew.

She threw her last ball. It knocked over all of the bottles, but one stood back up on its own.

"They're probably his slaves," she finished, referring to the interloper on the other side of the counter.

"I prefer to call them indentured laborers," said Shaydaway. Now standing right behind them, Zandria did not think he had enough time to walk all the way from the big tent. "Better luck next time," he added, referring to the lone standing bottle.

She thought her brain actually hurt. First, people started appearing and disappearing all over this carnival. Now Dew mentioned people coming from other dimensions. Zandria did not even know what that meant, but she did not like the sound of it. She wanted to ask questions to both Dew and Mister Shaydaway. She wanted to know what was happening at this twisted carnival. It was nothing like the annual Edge Town Faire back home.

Kez's words rang in hear ears, "Bad magic."

Zandria felt like she was getting used to the idea of magic. In Banookanook, she was never aware of being surrounded by it. However, whatever surrounded her right now made her feel completely helpless. Since her experience in the bell chamber at Castle Empyrean, she had felt truly connected to the castle, her sister and even somewhat to the other queens. Right now, she felt totally alone. The connection seemed to be there still, but it felt smothered under a pile of pillows. She wanted Dew's game with Shaydaway to be finished. She even thought running into the Blackwood Forest might be more appealing.

Then she had a feeling deep in her heart. It made her think of someone lighting a small candle inside a massive, dark cave. Zandria suddenly felt less alone. She had not thought about Adam in a while, but he was the candle in her moment of darkness. He was that bright spot in her heart. She knew he was on a mission with Prince William, but at this moment, she believed he was coming to her, giving her strength. In her mind, she saw him lying on an open field, staring up at millions of shining stars. He was safe and he was getting closer.

Zandria found new resolve, suddenly ready to finish the game.

"Do you have anything besides kiddy games?" she asked.

"Oh," Shaydaway leaned in close, "I have some delightfully terrible things to show you."

A few minutes ago, this statement would have sent Zandria running into the woods. Now, with her renewed confidence, she followed Shaydaway towards the main tent.

He pointed at one of the small tents on the side, "You may find this one interesting."

Zandria parted the curtain and cautiously poked in her head. A werewolf sprang at her. She stumbled back against Shaydaway. She could not believe he was blocking her escape. The werewolf stopped inches away from her. She could feel his warm, sticky breath on her face. She did not see it at first, but now saw the thick leather collar that held the growling beast chained to the pole in the center of the tent.

"Ka!" she said. It took all of her will, but Zandria did not let herself cry.

"I do apologize," said Shaydaway. "I get so turned around when we travel. I meant this tent over here." He gestured to a tent on the opposite side of the walkway. Dew offered her hand and Zandria took it as they moved to the next exhibit.

This time Zandria did cry. Inside the tent stood a unicorn. The mare could not move because each of her legs was cuffed right above the hooves with short chains attached to heavy-looking stakes pounded into the ground.

This unicorn made Shaydaway's tortured donkey look healthy. Broken at the tip, her golden horn held no shine and mucous dripped from her nose. Her blue eyes were watery and covered with a milky sheen. Dirt stained her pure white coat and she had a huge scar on her left flank. More dirt tangled and matted her tail and mane, while open sores oozed where the metal cuffs cut into her skin on all four legs.

As Zandria stared at this poor creature, she discovered that Shaydaway was far more evil than she imagined. She could not believe how anyone could do something like this. She promised herself that she would free the unicorn. It did not matter to her what Shaydaway wanted with her or Dew. She did not care why he sent Saman to find them or what his hidden purpose was. She swore, after she saved her mother, she would track down this traveling carnival of terror and save this poor creature.

Shaydaway, looking pleased with himself, steered them toward the main tent. He said, "Come. I want you to meet the rest of my family and have some refreshments."

He led them to the big top where Saman showed them to front row seats. The tent seemed much larger on the inside, but Zandria knew that had to be her imagination. She thought the illusion was caused by the rows of empty wooden benches lining the circular shape of the tent. While Shaydaway took center stage, Saman handed pewter cups to the girls, each filled to the top with a sweet smelling drink. Then he climbed up on a stool at the far side from them where he grabbed a box mounted atop a pole. Saman pulled a lever and a bright light flashed out at Mister Shaydaway. Zandria wondered how the light shone so brightly out of the wooden box Saman controlled until she was distracted by Shaydaway's *family members.*

To her right, Dew sipped the clear liquid.

"What is it?" Zandria asked, afraid it might be poison and already decided not to drink it.

"Wine," said Dew. "Dandelion, I think."

Zandria turned her attention back to the center where three figures waited in the shadows. As Shaydaway introduced them, Saman pointed the spot of light at each one.

"Ladies and gentlemen." He paused. "Perhaps, I should say, lady and lady. Normally, we don't perform for such a small audience. In any event, may I introduce our musical director, MacBeth."

The light shone on a man who looked more skeleton than flesh. His back hunched and the bone curved far out, stretching his gray-green skin. His arms were permanently bent in V-shapes with large, bulging elbows. The lower part of each of MacBeth's forearms was pierced with metallic rings and plates. If he did not look strange enough, Zandria noticed a gaping hole under his chin and another hole where his nose should have been.

Suddenly, MacBeth started an animated dance. His elbows banged on the stretched skin of his back like a big drum. The trinkets on his arms chimed like bells and he blew air through his chin hole like a flute. Zandria thought he was an entire band all by himself.

When MacBeth finished his short dance, Shaydaway said, "Next, may I present our star magician, Lazarou."

Lazarou looked like his face had been severely burned. His ashy, blackened skin showed cracks and he had no hair or eyebrows. Even his pupils were entirely black. He had no lips, but Zandria thought he tried to smile. Hiding the rest of his burnt skin, he wore a pink suit that looked like velvet. The pink, velvety suit covered what she imagined had to be a horribly scarred body. White gloves covered his hands, so Zandria could not be completely sure if he actually was burned on the rest of his body.

Lazarou held up his closed right fist. When he opened his hand, a small orange flame burst from it. The fire leapt up into the air and burned out instantly in a small show of his ability.

"And last, but never least, what carnival would be complete without a strong man?" announced Shaydaway. "Please welcome, Mister Gaunt."

The man definitely looked strong, Zandria thought. Wearing only some tight, short pants, his entire body bulged with muscles. He stood taller than the top of Shaydaway's tall hat. Zandria guess him to be near to eight or nine feet tall. None of these men made her feel any more comfortable. At least, she thought, they did not introduce any more tortured animals.

"At this point, the clowns and acrobats would come out," explained Shaydaway. "However, I suspect you are going to have a big day tomorrow, so you should get your rest. Please use my personal tent and I will see that someone tends to your horse."

Saman shut off the light and the four men in the center ring disappeared into darkness. The mutated dwarf did not even acknowledge the girls as he walked past them. Without speaking, they followed him to a lone tent behind the main one. The luxuriousness of Shaydaway's personal quarters impressed Zandria. So far, this private tent had been the only impressive thing at the carnival for her. She expected a simple cot or a blanket on the ground, but that night her and Dew shared a real bed with soft, warm blankets. Having this one pleasant thing did not make sleep any easier though.

Chapter 12

Adam Catches Up

Adam, Kalis and Crumb spent one night in Eisenhahn's clearing at the edge of the wasteland. Adam could barely take his eyes off the now shiny golden seagull as he waited to fall asleep. When he did look away, it was usually to check his reflection in the moonlit well for any signs of turning more copper. His hair did not feel any different, but he worried that he might end up like Eisenhahn, turning completely to metal.

Eisenhahn was the first to fall asleep that night. He snored loudly and that kept Adam awake. As Adam tried to fall asleep, he thought about the giant iron man. Despite his immense size, he acted like a child. Adam did not know if this meant there was something wrong with him or if he simply never learned anything being left alone to tend the passage his whole life. In either case, the big man seemed friendly and Adam felt a little sorry for him.

Crumb woke Adam early that morning as he flapped his wings. The seagull took off into the air, brightly reflecting the rising sun on his newly colored feathers. Eisenhahn did not wake up until after Adam had saddled Kalis. Adam saw a look of confusion on the iron man's face.

"Are you leaving?" asked Eisenhahn.

"That's right," said Adam.

Eisenhahn walked back toward the path into the jungle. "Then who will take care of this?"

Kalis said, "You will, I assume."

"Not if I'm coming with you."

Adam and Kalis looked at each other in surprise.

"I have a feeling there would be no stopping him," said Kalis.

"Well come on then," Adam said, waving an arm to Eisenhahn.

Eisenhahn started walking, a big grin spread across his face. He did not pack anything or check anything. He did not even ask any questions about where they were going.

They started out across the wasteland. When they left, Adam did not want anyone else to drink from the enchanted well, but none of them was able to write a warning sign. In case any thirsty travelers passed this way, Adam smashed the bucket to hopefully keep them out of the well. Soon they could not even see the clearing behind them.

Eisenhahn seemed really excited to be walking with them. His long legs always kept him a few paces ahead of Kalis. For the next couple of days, they moved across the uneven surface, dodging the occasional sinkhole. Crumb stayed vigilant, swooping down to warn them of each upcoming chasm.

As each day passed, Adam noticed the weather growing colder. He knew they were moving north and the soldier, Terg, warned them of the Ice Caps. Still, he spent his entire life in constant temperatures underground and did not know what to expect.

Then one morning, Adam woke up hoping to be greeted by the western sun. Instead, dull gray clouds filled the sky. There were also strange, wet flakes drifting out of the sky.

"I haven't seen snow for years," said Kalis.

Adam saw the flakes sticking to the Friesian's mane and tail. Sitting cross-legged on the ground, Eisenhahn looked up at the sky with his mouth open to catch the snow on his wide tongue.

This sudden cold made Adam not look forward to the coming days. He felt the crystal wanted him to avoid the Euphoric Mountains for a reason, but he did not know what that could be. His main concern now became cutting one of their blankets to make a coat.

As the day progressed, the snow flurry turned into a storm. Adam could not see more than a few feet in front of them, but he could feel them climbing upward. He wondered if they were actually heading into the mountains after all. He also saw no sign of Crumb and worried that the bird might be lost.

By the end of the day, the snowstorm stopped. With the last rays of the setting sun, the clouds cleared away and Adam spotted Crumb coming in for a landing.

It would be dark soon, so Adam wasted no time in digging a hole big enough for him and his companions. He believed it would be warmer down in the snow than exposed to the brutally cold wind. The unpacked snow moved easily as he used his long knife like a shovel. Eisenhahn, apparently thinking it was a game, joined the dig. His enormous hands quickly cleared away large piles. Soon the four of them were crowded around a small fire that Adam made from his blanket scraps and an empty saddlebag.

The ferocious night wind whistled over their heads. Waiting for sleep, Adam stared up into the clear sky. He still was not used to seeing stars overhead, but tonight they seemed especially bright. He figured it must be the cold, crisp air, but either the stars were closer or bigger than he had ever seen.

When he fell asleep, the sight of the glorious star-filled sky stayed in his head. As he lay on the ground, alone, he did not feel cold. The blowing wind had stopped in his dream. Adam lay still, surrounded by endless reaches of snow and blazing stars above him. He waited for something to happen.

Soon, as Adam hoped, something did happen. The stars began moving across the sky. At first, it seemed like darting in random directions. After a few moments, the stars had aligned themselves into a massive swirl and began spiraling inward. They moved faster and faster, growing together into one bright light at the center. When all of the millions of individual stars finished swirling together, a dark shape appeared in the center of the one massive star. He thought it was a tree, but like none he had ever seen. The tree looked short and fat. It looked as if a tangle of roots grew out of the top and the leafless branches stretched from the middle like wriggling tentacles.

Then Adam woke up.

There were no dismal clouds this morning. The sun, reflecting brightly off the miles of snow, hurt Adam's eyes. He tried not to look outward into the blinding white too much, but far off to his left, he did see the familiar purple and gray peaks of the Euphoric Mountains. He missed their warmth and shelter from this freezing wind. He realized that he probably would not have had his dream under the mountain's hypnotic influence. They had the power to make a person feel happy and forget the bad things, but that is not what he needed right now. He thought he understood why the crystal guided him away from them.

As they began their journey down the western side of the Ice Caps, Adam recounted his vision to Kalis.

The Friesian listened intently, then said, "It is like no tree I have seen, yet Vexwood Forest is a mysterious place. If we come across a tree like this, it may prove to be significant. It could possibly be our destination."

"Not if we go down there first," added Eisenhahn.

"What do you mean?" asked Adam, looking at the ground where the iron man pointed. A deep crack formed in the ice under them and grew wider with each of Kalis' hoof steps.

In an instant, the ice started splitting so fast that Adam knew they would be buried in its depths. Eisenhahn ran and Kalis kept pace at a full gallop. Each step starting a new split. The loud cracking and crashing surrounded them. A great chunk of ice snapped loose and burst up in front of them before sliding down into darkness. Adam saw the shiny layers that represented who knew how many years of falling snow.

With the next upheaval, Kalis reared up on his hind legs to avoid being hit. This threw Adam from the saddle.

He landed painfully on his back. He already did not like the snow. Now feeling how hard the soft-looking ice crystals were made him like it even less. He lay for a moment on a temporarily unmoving piece of ground. The fall knocked the breath out of him. In an instant, he could feel this patch begin to shake. Adam recovered and quickly rolled over, crawling as fast as he could to escape the widening chasm behind him. He could see the edge of this new collapse slightly out of reach in front of him. Kalis stood safely on solid ice, and Adam knew there was nothing the horse could do.

A second before he reached the safety of the Friesian, the frozen ground beneath him dropped into the hole.

Adam felt himself falling and knew he was finished. Then, he was not falling. He looked up to see Eisenhahn stretched over the ledge. Lying on his chest, the giant reached his long arm into the icy black pit. He held Adam by the wrist and pulled him to safety.

When Adam caught his breath, he said, "I'm definitely glad you came with us."

"Me too," said Eisenhahn with his boyish grin.

Adam studied the path behind them as he got to his feet. He saw the whole of the collapse center around where they were standing only a moment before. In a short distance to either side of that spot, the ground remained unmoved. It appeared to him that someone or something tried to target them. He voiced his suspicion to Kalis and Eisenhahn.

"Who would want to hurt me?" asked Eisenhahn.

Kalis said, "Precisely. Who would want to hurt any of us? It seems there may be some force determined to keep us from completing this task."

Adam saw the worried look on Eisenhahn's face and added, "Don't worry. I don't think there is anyone anywhere that would want to hurt you. They're after me and this crystal."

Adam quickly slapped his hand onto the crystal, expecting to find it secure in his waistband. For a moment, he feared it was gone, buried in that devouring crevasse. Then, relief washed over him as he felt its shape hidden beneath his shirt.

The iron man looked relieved by Adam's explanation.

"Then I will protect you and this crystal," said Eisenhahn.

Climbing onto Kalis' back, Adam smiled at Eisenhahn's sincerity. He did not think the man's simple mind understood exactly what they were trying to do. Instead, he believed the giant's thoughts were more basic and focused on his new friends and their immediate safety.

They spent one last night on the Ice Caps and before the next sunset, they were on dry ground. Adam could not have been happier to be clear of that frozen place. Although the air here still chilled him, he had never experienced cold like on the Ice Caps and never wanted to again. The fact that they did not experience any more ice quakes also improved his mood. He barely slept that last night for fear that he would wake up under tons of ice, if he woke up at all.

Now his thoughts focused on Eisenhahn's question of who was trying to stop them. As they made their way down the tundra toward the looming Vexwood Forest, Adam discussed it with Kalis. Their consensus was that these crystals, however many there were, formed some type of prison. Adam decided that whoever trapped Zandria's mother in the crystal was very powerful and also very dangerous.

Kalis stopped to nibble at one of the scarce stunted shrubs. He said, between bites, "If the queen's mother has only been missing for six years, it is very likely that our villain is still waiting and watching." He paused. "Mind you, I say villain because we are assuming whoever did this, did this for less than honorable purposes."

"Sounds like a villain to me," said Adam. "I don't think it's Lord Vanril or the witch, Sasha. I never heard them talk about anything like this."

"Yet, you did find your crystal in their lair," responded Kalis.

"It feels bigger than them," said Adam. "Maybe it is part of a trap for all four queens."

"As such, five or six or even ten years would not be too long for someone to wait," said Kalis. "Your finding the crystal and following its instructions could be quite upsetting to our mysterious villain."

Kalis started in the direction of the waiting tree line. Adam figured they would be entering Vexwood shortly after dark. The closer they got, the better Adam could see the forest. The more detail he could make out, the less he wanted to be there after dark.

There was not one particular thing about Vexwood Forest that Adam did not like. It proved to be an overall feeling of uneasiness. The woods were not bleak and lifeless like the Dead Forest through which he tracked Zandria and Olena. This forest seemed very much alive. There was movement, slithery sneaking movement, behind the tangles of branches.

Once inside the forest, Adam could not believe Kalis said, "It's good to be home."

Eisenhahn said what Adam was thinking before he could get it out, "You like it here?"

"Well," Kalis corrected himself, "no Friesian likes Vexwood and rarely does anyone from Castlewood venture this far east. What I meant was that it was good to be back in the Northern Wood."

"I don't like it here," said Eisenhahn. He kept looking into the woods on either side of the narrow path, brushing low-hanging branches out of his face with one big hand.

Adam did not like it here either. There was no light from the moon or stars. With every step, it kept getting darker, but Adam could still feel things moving around them. He knew their situation would seem better in the daylight, if daylight could penetrate this murky place.

He asked, "How far do you plan on going tonight?"

"There is supposed to be a human settlement near the eastern edge. I don't know how close we are though," said Kalis.

Every time Adam felt ready to stop for the night, Kalis insisted on going a little further, that the village must be close. Adam began to suspect the horse was not telling him something about this forest. He could feel eyes watching him from all sides and there were continuous hissing noises coming from the underbrush. Adam believed if he turned around in the saddle, some hideous creature would be waiting right behind him. For that reason, he kept his eyes focused on the darkness ahead of him.

Soon the black of night turned into a dim gray sunrise and then into a bright gray morning.

"Finally," said Kalis, "we can stop anywhere you want now."

"What are you talking about?" asked Adam.

"It's bad luck to talk about it at night, but it's worse luck to sleep in this wood at night. It is slightly safer in the day."

"So, no village then?" asked Adam, already knowing the answer.

"I'm afraid not," said Kalis. "I apologize for the misinformation, but I needed to give you a reason to keep going. I didn't want one of us to fall under a spell or disappear while we were sleeping. How do you think this place got its name?"

Adam looked around in the dim light trying to fight its way through the haze above him. He could see nothing moving now, but sensed a few creatures nearby, probably still watching them. In this light, the trees looked dark red and the sickly leaves were various shades of red, orange and pale white.

Eisenhahn said, "Look, a clearing."

Adam and Kalis turned their attention ahead of them. The path did open into a clearing. It did not look as big as Eisenhahn's old home, but Adam was glad not to have the forest pressing in on him. The only thing that made him feel better about their potential campsite was the tree at the center of the small field. It was the same twisted tree from his dream.

The tree was dark red, almost maroon, like the rest of the wood around them. Almost as wide as it was tall, the tree stood a little shorter than Eisenhahn. The strange roots growing out of the top twisted and curved in every direction. And like in his dream, several thick branches grew out of the middle of the trunk at about his own head height. A chill ran up Adam's back as he watched those leafless branches writhing with no wind blowing.

Adam slipped down out of the saddle and moved toward the tree, almost hypnotized by its swaying. A loud "Scrawt" broke his trance. Adam spun around to see Crumb resting on a branch of an apple tree that looked unusually healthy in this forest. He forgot that the seagull took off without them last night. Relieved to see the gold bird safe from this frightening place, he waved at him.

Turning back to the tree, Adam noticed something that he missed a moment ago. Surrounding the base of the tree were small holes in the ground. It disturbed him that these holes appeared to be lined with jagged, wooden teeth. Adam realized that the moving branches could have easily swept him in to be plant food for the waiting mouths. He also realized that Crumb helped him once again. If not for the bird's call, he may not have noticed the mouths.

He turned back to thank Crumb and saw the seagull about to peck at one of the strangely shiny apples.

"Don't!" shouted Kalis. "That's a poison apple tree." Kalis trotted over to Crumb. He explained, "Don't eat anything in this place. I am in no mood to kiss a sleeping bird."

Adam laughed at this and the sound of his voice echoed through the wood. A few eerie titters and cackles answered him back. This did not make Adam feel better.

Then Eisenhahn said, "I think it's on fire."

Kalis and Adam moved to Eisenhahn's side of the grotesque tree. In the middle of the trunk, Adam saw a hollow and inside, as the big man said, a fire burned. Then Adam saw something else engulfed in the flames dancing inside the tree.

"It's another crystal," he almost shouted.

As Adam stared into the flames, he had the inexplicable feeling that Zandria was in trouble. An uncontrollable sense of urgency took over his mind. This caused him to charge for it before Kalis could say, "Wait."

Adam stepped over one of the snapping tree mouths and jabbed his hand into the hole. He snatched it back quickly from the heat without grabbing the crystal.

"What were you thinking?" Kalis scolded Adam.

While they were looking at each other, Eisenhahn stuck in his enormous arm and grabbed the crystal. Apparently, Adam discovered, his iron skin was not affected by the flames.

Eisenhahn handed the rapidly cooling crystal to Adam and said, "Here you go. I told you I would take care of you. I'm good at taking care of things."

Chapter 13

The Fourth Crystal

Uneasy sleep turned into unpleasant dreams and morning could not come soon enough for Zandria.

Awake and out of bed before Dew, Zandria went outside. She found Tihi being groomed by Saman. The dwarf brushed the horse, precariously balanced on a short ladder. She did not think this would be an effective technique as Saman kept wobbling back and forth. He spent more time shifting his weight and watching the ground than actually brushing.

Zandria took over for him without a word and he went about his other morning duties. Soon, Dew joined her. She quickly saddled Tihi.

"Are you ready to head into the forest?" asked the elf as she tightened the straps under Tihi's belly.

"Don't you want to have breakfast with your new friends?" Zandria said facetiously.

"We're not going to talk about that right now." Dew turned away and finished checking their saddlebags.

Then Zandria felt the sun on her back suddenly vanish. She turned around to find Shaydaway standing right behind her, blocking the morning warmth. There was no sound of him walking. One moment, he was not there and the next, he was. Zandria did not think she could get used to someone who did that all the time.

"Oh," she said.

"And a wonderful morning to you," he replied. Mister Shaydaway seemed to be dressed in the same clothes from yesterday, but they were as clean and smooth as a brand new suit. He must have a trunk full of the same outfit, Zandria guessed.

He continued, "I trust you will be ready for breakfast momentarily."

"We're leaving," said Zandria.

"Not running off into that nasty little forest so soon, are we?" Zandria did not like this stranger knowing where they were going.

"We're looking for herbs," Dew lied. "My grandmother is sick."

"Oh, I see," said Shaydaway. He leaned in close to the girls. "If you should happen to find anything that you think might interest me, I will be close." Then he stood back up and, in his best theatrical voice, said, "The Carnivale Chaotica is on an extensive engagement of the Northern Woods."

Shaydaway strolled off and Zandria stared at his back. Zandria could think of nothing good about this man or his traveling nightmare show. He knew where they were coming from and where they were going to. He even hinted at knowing they were looking for something other than Dew's pretend herbs. For now, the thing she disliked about him most was that he had a unicorn prisoner.

Dew mounted Tihi, then pulled Zandria up on the back of the saddle. As they rode past the carnival, Zandria saw the interlopers starting to unstake the tents and take apart the booths.

"They're leaving," said Tihi. "The donkey told me they almost never stay in the same place more than one night."

"I hope never to see them again," said Zandria.

"I don't think we'll have much choice," said Dew.

"What does that mean?" asked Zandria.

Before Dew could answer, they passed Shaydaway's wagon. He stood on the back door stairs and Lazarou stood on the ground. Zandria thought she heard the magician say something in his crusty voice about collapsing ice..

"Our ice trap did not succeed," he hissed.

Then the two men turned to the girls and slowly waved goodbye. Dew nudged Tihi to the right and the horse turned to head into Blackwood Forest. Zandria kept her eyes on

Shaydaway to make sure he did not follow them. An oily, black tree momentarily blocked her vision. When she could see him again, Shaydaway was now seated on his high bench and Lazarou was nowhere to be seen. She looked through the other scattered trees and could see no signs of the rest of the carnival. She could not believe they were packed already.

The last time Zandria saw Shaydaway that day, he started whipping the donkey and they rolled away in the opposite direction. The Carnivale Chaotica must be moving on to their next performance, she thought. Being rid of them gave her a temporary feeling of relief that faded as Blackwood Forest surrounded them.

After they were deep into Blackwood, Dew finally spoke. "You have to learn some patience," she said.

"What does that mean?"

"It means all of your questions could have waited. In case you didn't notice, that man was evil. I'm talking peel-your-skin-off-evil," said Dew.

"That's what I was trying to tell you," said Zandria with frustration. "I could tell he was bad."

"Yes, but you can't say that to his face. That's like asking to be boiled alive."

Zandria asked, "What was I supposed to do?"

"Like I said, we didn't have a choice," explained Dew. "He was looking for us. I'm sure he's something more than an entertainer. Maybe he sensed you and the crystal coming close.

People like that are always trying to find new magic."

"I hate to interrupt your debate, but does anyone know where we're going?" asked Tihi. This whole time, the Friesian made her own course as they wandered deeper into the forest.

"Don't ask me," said Dew. "I can't see anything other than barren fields."

Zandria forgot that elves could not see Blackwood. Being surrounded by the dangling leaves and grease-stained bark, she could not even imagine seeing anything else.

"I don't know where we're going either. There might not even be another crystal here," said Zandria.

"Well, this was your idea," said Dew.

"That doesn't mean I know where we're going."

"That doesn't surprise me," said Dew. "Humans are too stupid. You probably had a hard time finding your way out of the tent this morning."

"That was mean," said Zandria.

"You think so? Then try this." Dew twisted around and pulled Zandria's hair.

"Ow!"

Zandria pulled back her fist to hit Dew, but Tihi reared up on her hind legs first. Both girls hit the ground hard.

"Stop it, both of you," demanded Tihi. "You're acting like unbridled fillies."

Dew and Zandria sat silently on the ground looking up at the Friesian. Zandria noticed for the first time how quiet Blackwood was. She did not hear the chirp of even a single bird.

Tihi continued, "Maybe it's this place, but I would have expected better from the queen's sister and especially one of the Lantisphere clan."

"Sorry, Tihi," Dew said.

"Don't tell me," answered Tihi.

Dew turned to Zandria, but looked down at the ground. She barely mumbled her apology.

"Me too," said Zandria.

Tihi circled Dew and nudged her toward Zandria. The girls helped each other off the ground. Disappointed at her own behavior, Zandria could not bring herself to say anything else at the moment. To avoid eye contact, she bent over to brush off the dirt from her fall. As she stood up, the crystal fell from her pocket.

She instinctively reached for it, but the crystal started to glow bright white. Dew pulled her back. Zandria watched the glowing shard start to spin like a compass needle. Finally, it stopped, settling on a direction slightly west of their original course. Then the crystal skidded through the dirt leaving a definite indication of which way they should go. After that, the light faded and Zandria moved to gingerly grab it. It surprised her that it was not at all hot.

"I guess we know which way now," said Zandria.

Then Dew slapped a hand over her mouth. Zandria could not speak through the soft skin of the slender elven fingers, but she figured Dew must still be mad at her. She wanted to know why the elf was holding her. She could not believe Dew wanted to continue the fight this way.

Then Tihi whispered, "I hear it, too." She turned her head and lifted up her black ears.

Dew whispered to Zandria, cool lips brushing her earlobe. Zandria's urge to laugh at the tickling sensation faded when she processed the single word, "Werewolf."

The girls hurriedly climbed onto Tihi and the horse bolted in the direction the crystal pointed. Zandria saw Tihi purposely use her hoof to smear away the line in the dirt that might give away their path. They rode fast and Zandria fought her fear. Dew had not said anything about werewolves in this forest, so the only one she could think of was the one at the carnival. Maybe, she thought, it escaped. The she realized it was more likely that Shaydaway sent the wolfman to follow them.

After a short while, Dew said, "I can still hear him. He's farther away, but his chains are rattling nice and loud."

"Do you think he's coming to hurt us?" Zandria could only think of her last encounter with a werewolf. The wolf man that killed her father definitely wanted to hurt her in the bell chamber of Empyrean. Zandria had not gained enough compassion from Empyrean's magic yet to feel anything but hate for werewolves.

"Probably a spy," said Dew. "Shaydaway must know what we're after. He's not brave enough to get it himself, so he'll probably try to find us once we have it."

Tihi slowed to a walk again. The trees were getting closer and the ground was turning to muck. Zandria saw they had no choice as the horse struggled to pull her hooves out of the mud.

"What do you think he wants it for?" she asked.

"There's no question he's a magic user. You saw how he controlled those interlopers. The question is whether he learned about the crystal from reading your mind or if he was already looking for it," explained Dew.

Zandria did not like the thought of someone reading her mind. If that was possible, then none of her secrets or feelings would be private. She distracted herself from that unpleasant possibility by asking about the interlopers.

"You said the interlopers come from other dimensions. What is a dimension?"

Dew looked annoyed by the sudden change in topic, but answered, "Do you think this is the only world that exists? Well, there are more realities than you could imagine. Sometimes people cross over. Some on purpose, others fall through a tear on accident. If they don't make it all the way through or back to their own world, then they get stuck and become an interloper. Their body and spirit are torn between both worlds without a true existence in either."

This idea amazed and stunned her. Zandria was only now beginning to experience the world outside of Banookanook. She could not comprehend that anything could exist beyond the four queendoms of Empyrean. She suspected these worlds were much farther away than even trying to cross the sea back home.

"Can we get back on topic here?" asked Dew.

"Sorry. It's so hard to believe," said Zandria.

"It's not something you'll ever have to worry about. Your worries are chasing us right now," said Dew. "When we find this crystal, we need to get back to Truewood without running into that carnival. Unfortunately, I think we are closer to Castlewood Forest now."

"That means we'll have to cross the valley," added Tihi.

"And that means wood spirits," finished Dew.

Zandria wanted to ask about the wood spirits, but something else caught her attention. Tihi walked into a small glade. In the center, hanging in mid-air, Zandria saw another crystal.

Dew stopped talking and turned to face Zandria, apparently waiting for another question. When she saw Zandria's expression, she turned in that direction. Even if she could not see the forest, she must have been able to see the crystal.

"What are you waiting for? Let's get it," she said.

Zandria looked at their surroundings. At first, she thought Tihi could ride over and she could snatch it out of the air. Then she looked closer at the dirt and black leaves covering the ground beneath it. Something seemed strange about the way the leaves gently waved over the apparently solid ground.

She dropped down from Tihi's back and took a few steps toward the crystal. Zandria knelt down and examined the ground. She stuck out her fingers and they sank through what she thought should be solid dirt. Under the surface, the ground felt wet like the mud back behind them, only more watery. Suddenly her hand sank in up to her wrist and she could feel it sucking at her. Zandria looked around for something to hold onto, but found nothing. She knew it could only be a matter of seconds before she was pulled under the surface.

"Help me," she called.

Dew sprang from Tihi and grabbed Zandria by her free arm. She pulled once and could not get Zandria free. When she relaxed her grip, Zandria sank in up to her elbow.

"Hurry!"

"I'm trying," said Dew.

The elf pulled one more time. Zandria watched her face turn red from the strain. Then Zandria could feel herself slipping loose. She broke free and fell back into Dew. The two girls collapsed on top of each other. Zandria hugged Dew tightly.

"Thank you. Thank you."

"Okay. You're welcome. I can't breathe," said Dew.

Zandria let go and they got to their feet. Dew moved close to the spot where Zandria almost sank.

"Wait. That's too close," she said.

"It's okay. I should have noticed it before," said Dew. "The whole area beneath the crystal is sabelsifi."

"Sabel-what?" asked Zandria.

"Sabelsifi," answered Tihi. "It roughly means dirt water. It's not very common, but very fast and very dangerous. If you went in any further, then there would have been nothing we could do."

Dew started walking in a circle around the crystal. She never moved close enough to where they could reach it even on Tihi's back.

She said, "You want to know something funny, Zandria? Some people believe sabelsifi marks a passage to other dimensions."

Zandria did not think this was very funny. First, she did not like the thought of being so close to drowning or suffocating. She was not sure what would happen to a person under that stuff. Then to think it might be a passage to another dimension scared her even more. She did not want to be in another world all alone, or worse, trapped in between in something like this.

"What a horrible way to travel," she said.

Dew laughed at this and that made Zandria feel a little better.

"I have a suggestion for getting the crystal," said Tihi. "I'm afraid you won't be much help with this, Dew."

"What's your thought?" asked Zandria, eager to hold the crystal.

Tihi answered, "Some of these trees look rotten. Maybe I could knock one down across the sabelsifi. Then all you have to do is walk across."

"This could be interesting," said Dew.

Zandria said, "Let's try it."

It only took a few minutes to find a tree wide enough. Tihi moved behind it and pushed with her hind legs. Dew stood back, unable to see what was happening. The tree cracked at its base and toppled. Zandria waited for it to hit the ground, but that never happened. Instead, the tree slammed against one on the other side and wedged in its branches.

"No," shouted Zandria.

"What? Tell me what happened," said Dew.

"The tree got stuck," said Tihi. "She can still walk on it, but she'll be up high above the sabelsifi. On the bright side, the crystal will be easier to reach."

Zandria did not want to balance on that oily wood. She knew if she fell, there would be nothing to grab on to. She looked around fearing the werewolf would be close.

"Let's try another one," she suggested, when she did not see their pursuer.

"Shhh," said Dew.

"But," started Zandria.

"It's the werewolf," whispered Dew.

Zandria froze. In the quiet of the forest, she could hear the faint clinking of chains coming closer. Dew stared into the distance.

"I see him," she said. Zandria looked in the same direction, but could only see the lifeless black trees. She discovered one definite advantage for Dew not being able to see Blackwood.

"Ha," Dew continued. "I guess werewolves can't see Blackwood either."

"Why?" asked Tihi, searching for him also.

"He keeps tripping and banging into things that must be trees."

"That means he can probably see us, as well," said Tihi.

Dew put her hands on her hips and shook her head. She sighed, "We're going to have one mad werewolf when he finally gets here."

Tihi shepherded Zandria toward their fallen tree. She said, "There's no time. You have to use this one."

Zandria looked up the slope of the wood. Her stomach turned like it did when she climbed down the wall of the canyon to get into Castle Empyrean. She put her hands on the trunk and it felt as slimy as she imagined it would. Then she took her first step. Her foot slipped on the oil exuding from the tree, but thankfully hit solid ground. She started again and found a solid footing. With each step up the angle of the tree, she rose higher over the sabelsifi.

"He's getting closer," said Dew.

This did not help Zandria concentrate, but, finally, she made it up over the center. All she had to do was reach out and grab the crystal. She thought, after that, she could easily slide back down the fallen tree. She stretched out her hand and the crystal hung barely beyond her fingertips. She was afraid to reach any farther in case she lost her balance.

Dew screamed, "He's here!"

Then the werewolf exploded through the branches. Zandria felt wet splinters hit her leg.

He leapt straight towards her, sailing through the air over the sabelsifi. Everything seemed to move in slow motion to Zandria. She saw every sharp tooth in his wide-open mouth. She saw the leather collar with its trailing broken chain and knew for certain he came from the Carnival Chaotica.

As he flew closer, Zandria's vision went black. At first, she thought she was fainting, but then she clearly saw Adam. He stood by a giant metal man, holding two crystals. Then she heard her mother's voice, "Four into one."

Zandria now knew this was the fourth crystal and lunged for it. As she grabbed it, she lost her balance and fell. The wolfman's momentum carried him over the tree and he fell to the ground at the edge of the sabelsifi. The false ground sucked his hind legs under instantly. Zandria dangled from the tree, her legs crossed and wrapped tightly around the trunk. By the time she shimmied down to safety, the sabelsifi completely pulled the wolfman beneath the surface.

Dew helped Zandria away from the edge of the sabelsifi. They sat on safe ground and Zandria held her two crystals side by side. They were identical and she knew Adam had two more exactly the same. She did not know where Adam was or how to make the four into one as her mother and Olena instructed. Her main concern now was getting back to Truewood or Castlewood without an encore performance from Raymond Shaydaway and his Carnivale Chaotica.

Chapter 14

The Trip to Bremen

The coldness of Soria Moria seeped over William. He shivered under his baggy shirt that should have overlapped enough to keep him warm. The Bondsfolk were kind enough to give him some clothes in his new size. Before he left Bond, they opened the storeroom where they put their missing children's belongings, trying to hide it from their own memory. Still, he hoped to himself that staying in his own clothes might somehow slow his reverse aging.

Aleta did not seem affected by the cold, although she still wore her traditional two-piece uniform. Before they reached Bond, on the windy expanse of wasteland, Terg asked her why she barely covered herself. She explained that her body was as much of a weapon as her spear and could not be restricted by something like clothes. William knew little of the southern lands, but he knew it was hot. He wondered how she could stand the cold on her bare bronze-colored skin.

He led Aleta into the darkened front hall of the towering castle while the two Friesians waited outside. All of Soria Moria seemed darker now than the last time he walked its halls. William guessed with the release of the two ghostly princesses, the castle really was empty. Without the miniature wooden butler, Sylvan, no one remained to care for the ancient structure.

They had to light torches to continue down the main hall that encircled the tower. William tried to remember where the archive room might be. He had only been in Soria Moria a few times. It started to sink in that the last time was five hundred years ago and he had almost no memory of it now.

On the side of the castle furthest from the main gate, they passed a wide staircase that led down into the catacombs. William suspected that would be a perfect place for a troll's nest.

"I believe it's empty now, but I would not suggest going down there," he said.

"Why?" asked Aleta.

"Trolls," came William's one word answer.

He looked back to see how she would react. Her unimpressed expression made William think that nothing existed in Empyrean that could scare her. Every day that he spent with Aleta gave him a new respect for the people of the Southern Valley. If they were all like her, then they were a formidable people, especially their women.

She said, "I have heard of this, these trolls. They do not sound so big. We have many creatures much larger in my country."

William remembered trolls being three or four times bigger than his normal size. He did not like the idea of anything that made a troll seem not so big. Then he found a wooden door twisted askew off its hinges and that distracted him from his troll concerns.

Aleta helped him pry the jammed door out of its frame. Without the assistance of the broken hinges, the wood crashed to the floor. The noise echoed down the hall, bounced around the circle of the entire castle and came back to them from the other direction.

Inside, William found the room he wanted. The Archive of Soria Moria had been untouched for hundreds of years. He could not imagine why so much precious information would have been left here to rot.

"Why did they not take this with them?" he said aloud.

William did not expect a response from Aleta, but she said, "Maybe they thought the trolls would protect it."

That seemed reasonable to William. Then he considered that the trolls were the reason they did not take it in the first place. It occurred to him that, more likely, the humans escaped Soria Moria as opposed to moved. So here, the history of the queendom of the Eastern Sky remained buried.

Sorting through the books and scrolls took most of the day. William saw every type of text he could imagine. Purposefully, he avoided reading anything that mentioned his queen. Finally, he found the Fountainhead Compendium, the complete history of his hometown. William flipped through the pages. It stung to see himself on the pages being knighted as protector of his village and the territory. He skipped the part about his betrothed becoming queen. On the last page of the thin book, in a different handwriting, were the words "Fountainhead shall henceforth be known as Frostwick."

This information unlocked that cold part of his heart. A chilly breeze flicked at their torches. For Aleta's sake, if not his own, he quickly reined in his emotions. He did not know why the broken pieces of his heart caused his original freeze, but he did not want that to happen again. He suspected his aging problem had something to do with his lonely heart as well.

Instead of letting the sadness take him, he focused on sorting through the information about his town of two names. Without mentioning him or the cause, the books alluded to a sudden cold that started freezing the forest. Because the ice did not rapidly cover the land, people continued to live in the area and the town of Fountainhead eventually became known as Frostwick due to its constantly chilly climate.

From there, William searched for the Frostwick Compendium. In it, he scoured family records until he found Adam's parents. He did not know how he could tell Adam that both of them were lost in a fire when he was only a baby. William suspected the fire must have been started by the dwarves that kidnapped Adam.

Aleta insisted they keep reading. She hoped maybe they would come across another close relative still alive in Bond. What they found was a relative, but none for which William could ever have been prepared. He traced the singular family tree back through the generations, quickly establishing the boy had no living relatives. Aleta read the name of Adam's great, great, great, great grandmother aloud, "Mia".

This woman's name had no meaning for William, but her parents' names caused him to drop the book he held. Adam's five times great grandparents had the same names as William's parents five hundred years ago. William could not believe what Aleta read to him. He scanned the documents and saw quickly that Adam was, without a doubt, his great, great, great, great, great nephew.

Since William never had any children of his own, that meant Mia had to be a sister he never met. William dreaded the possibility that he might be getting used to disappointment and loss. When he retreated to his fountain garden, he not only lost his love, but a baby sister as well. He let sadness and hopelessness steal his life away back then. Already, he knew Adam was a special boy. Now, he was the only person William had in this changed world. He could not lose hope again.

William led Aleta out of the Archive with a renewed sense of purpose. He fulfilled his promise to Adam and in doing so gained a family. He smiled when he thought about looking up to the probably taller Adam and telling him the news. How funny it would be to have an uncle younger than himself, William thought. His heart truly felt happy and light for the first time in five hundred years.

When William and Aleta made it outside, they found the horses startled. Both Friesians were looking to the south with pricked up ears and swishing tails. Sulis looked barely able to stand still.

Then the thing that startled them burst out of the bushes. Terg and the youngest Smoltz Brother charged at them with swords drawn. William quickly surmised the men were not charging, but retreating.

Coming at a full run, Terg shouted, "Into the castle. Bar the gate."

"We can't, it's broken," answered William with a growing sense of urgency.

"They're right behind us," yelled Smoltz, looking over his shoulder, presumably for signs of their pursuers.

"I see no one," started Aleta. Then two massive Rockhorns smashed through the trees. Their pointed heads lowered like charging beasts, they swung their weapon shaped hands to clear their path.

William and Aleta quickly followed Terg and Smoltz back into Soria Moria. Without the iron door to protect them, they chose to barricade themselves in the great hall. William could definitely hear more than one werewolf now growling on the other side and the dwarf Vanril ordering, "Break it down."

Terg dropped onto one of the dusty, overstuffed couches. He looked exhausted and heaved like he could not catch his breath. Through gasps, he said, "We found him."

"I can see that," said William, standing in front of Terg. He felt like a little boy waiting to sit on his grandfather's lap. "Where's your brother?" he asked the remaining Smoltz.

"The wolfmen ambushed us," said Smoltz, fighting off tears for his apparently lost brother.

"We had him," complained Terg. "If I had my long bow, this would already have been finished. The runt was heading east, in the direction of the palace. He met up with some friends."

"When are you going to tell me something I don't know?" asked William, referring to the Rockhorns and wolfmen.

Terg stared at him. "Maybe if you had kept your word and helped me, we would not be trapped here right now."

"I'm sorry," said William, "but sorry does not win battles. We must deal with what's in front of us and determine a strategy."

They quickly checked their weapons and possible escape routes. The whole time, the Rockhorns pounded on the door. William thought the old wood held surprisingly well. He thought to check for the Taenarum Tunnel that aided his escape last time he was here, but found no sign of it.

With no chance of escape, they finally decided on a plan.

"Then we make a stand here," said William. "For the Northern Wood."

"And the Eastern Sky," added Terg.

They dumped tables on their sides and arranged the couches to provide the best wall of defense they could. William knew the furniture barricade would not hold for long. Then the Rockhorns smashed through the door.

The two stone brutes lumbered in, breaking the furniture to splinters. Three werewolves bounded in next. One met a sudden end at the tip of Aleta's spear. The other two came for William and Terg. Sulis back-kicked one of the wolfmen into the other and they both slid across the stone floor. Vanril came in last, picked a target and hurled a small dagger directly at young Smoltz's neck.

At the last second, Terg blocked the dagger with the only thing he could, his chest. The blade sank in deep and Terg staggered for a moment. He caught himself and pulled the dagger out of his chest. When Vanril saw this, he turned to run.

William had no intention of failing Terg again, so he started to chase the dwarf. Then the floor shook beneath their feet. Everyone stopped fighting for a moment, but nothing else happened. The fighting resumed when one of the werewolves clawed Smoltz on the arm. Terg chopped down that wolfman with his sword and Aleta finished the other.

William started to go after Vanril again. The two humongous Rockhorns moved to block his passage. The floor shook a second time and William thought it must be the Rockhorn's movements. Then it shook a third time when the Rockhorn were not moving.

"Trolls," William said, stifling a grin. He never imagined being happy about trolls. A club the size of one of the Rockhorns burst up through the floor. As it pulled back down, both Rockhorns fell into the new hole. "There are still trolls downstairs," William finished over the horrible sounding troll moans coming from the black pit. Apparently, he thought, the trolls did not like all the noise being made above them.

Aleta helped William bring Terg and Smoltz outside, away from the trolls.

They sat the wounded down in the grass with the two Friesians keeping watch for any more attackers. William looked at Smoltz's arm. The scratch looked deep, but not life threatening.

"Will I turn into one of them?" asked Smoltz, obviously afraid of the answer.

"They are vicious beasts, but not contagious," William reassured him. Then he moved to Terg. The old soldier did not look like he would last much longer. William said, "You saved Smoltz's life."

"Good," whispered Terg. "Did you get Vanril?"

"You have my word," said William, not completely answering the question.

"Then I can return home with honor." Apparently, Terg could manage no more than a whisper. Then he faded away. The wound to Terg's chest did not look too serious, but the black liquid surrounding it told William the dagger was poisoned.

William knelt by the body of the soldier for a moment longer. Finally, he said, "Aleta, would you make sure these two get back to Castle Empyrean and arrange a hero's funeral for Terg?"

He stood up, pulled off his oversized shirt and laid it across Terg's vacant face. William sorted through the saddlebags for clothes more his size. He also traded his sword for a knife more suited to his smaller hand.

"What are you going to do?" asked Aleta.

William scanned the ground for Vanril's tracks into the forest. He knew the dwarf was heading in the direction of the animal town of Bremen. He said, "I'm going to keep my promise."

Chapter 15

The Long Way Home

Adam turned the crystal over in his hands, still warm from the flames inside the bizarre looking tree. He glanced at Eisenhahn, who looked overjoyed that he could help. Then he turned back to the newly found crystal. He saw an image deep inside it, rushing toward him.

The woman he guessed to be Zandria's mother appeared again. He forgot the impact she had on his feelings. When he saw her beauty, he wanted only to be with his own mother although he did not know what she looked like. This thought brought him to the verge of crying and he wanted to abandon this quest yet again. Knowing he could help someone else, especially Zandria, find her own mother kept him on course.

This time, the woman did not look directly at him or call his name. Instead, she simply said, "Four into one."

"Is that supposed to help?" asked Kalis, leaning in over Adam's shoulder.

Adam looked back at the horse for a moment and then turned to the crystal, hoping for more instructions. However, the woman said nothing else. As she started fading away, his overwhelming fear that Zandria was in trouble returned. Looking deep into the crystal, almost like looking through it to somewhere else, he saw a horrifying scene that lasted for only an instant.

It felt like looking down a long straight tunnel and at the far end, he could see Zandria. She clung to an ugly, black tree with a look of fear in her eyes. He thought he saw a werewolf lunging at her. Then the image disappeared.

"Did you see that?" he asked Kalis.

"See what?" responded the Friesian.

"Zandria's in trouble."

Eisenhahn tapped Adam on the shoulder. "I think we're in trouble too."

Adam looked around to see what spooked the big man. Rapidly filling their small clearing, strange creatures completely surrounded them despite their apparent dislike for the hazy sunlight. At first, they seemed adorable, shielding the light with their tiny hands, but then Adam noticed their sharp teeth and claws. Some of them disappeared and then reappeared in different spots in puffs of magical smoke. Some of them turned into to snakes or rats and then back into the small, two-legged creatures that seemed to be their natural form. Some were furry and some were hairless, but everyone had a look of evil in each of their three eyes.

"I knew this was too easy," said Kalis. "These are curses. Keep your mouth closed no matter what."

Then the menacing creatures swarmed. Eisenhahn stomped on a few with his large feet and they squished beneath his weight. After that, they had no chance. The curses flooded over them. One even jumped on Crumb's back as he tried to fly from his branch. In an instant, the entire clearing became a tussling and turning mass of curses.

The crystals did nothing for Zandria. She got no visions, messages or signs. She sat on the damp ground, staring at the sabelsifi. She hoped the wolfman did not cross over into someone else's world. She did not want to be responsible for causing anyone else pain. She knew it could not be possible, but she thought the monster might burst up out of the ground at any moment, coming back to get her.

He did not.

Dew held a whispered conversation with Tihi while Zandria tried to recover. From the bits she heard, she knew they were planning a route out of Blackwood. Dew came back and sat next to Zandria.

"No hurry, but are you ready to go yet?" asked the elf.

"I'm not getting anything," said Zandria. She wanted guidance from her mother. She wanted the crystals to light up and tell her what to do next.

Dew sounded sympathetic, "We really should be moving. I don't see anyone else coming, but I don't think staying here is a good idea."

Zandria wished she was an elf right now. She would gladly not have to look at these thick oily black trees and their sagging, weeping branches. She felt that staying close to the crystal's home might help her contact her mother one more time. Still, she did not want to stay here any longer either.

Dew stood and offered her hand. Zandria took it and pulled herself from the ground. They stood face to face, then Dew gave Zandria a ferocious hug. She squeezed so hard, this time, Zandria ran out of breath.

"What was that for?" she asked when they parted.

"I'm happy you're safe. That's all," said Dew. "And I wanted to tell you thanks."

She cupped her hands and bent over next to the Friesian. Zandria could not believe Dew was letting her mount Tihi first. Climbing onto the front of the saddle, Zandria said, "Thanks for what?"

The elf climbed up behind her. She said, "Thanks for trusting me with this. You don't know how boring it is in Truewood. I mean, I'm almost fifty and they still treat me like a child. After we get these crystals back, that should prove my worth to my clan. By the way, where are we taking these crystals?"

Surprised by Dew's emotional release, Zandria had to think of her answer. "To Castle Empyrean, I guess. We have to find Adam, first. He has the other two," she said.

"Where is he?" asked Tihi, as she carried them away from the sabelsifi.

"I'm not sure," said Zandria. "I think he's close."

"Then, I think we are closer to Castlewood. Heading for the safety of the castle may be our best plan. Don't forget Raymond Shaydaway is out here somewhere," said Dew.

Tihi and Zandria agreed and they began to make their way out of Blackwood.

Tihi wound through the forest that only she and Zandria could see. Before long, they were on a narrow ridge. To the east and west, Zandria could see the ridge open up to a grazing plain like the one where they first found the carnival. Then she remembered, they did not find the carnival, it found them. The thought of that tall, skinny man sent shivers down her spine even in the bright afternoon sun.

At the edge of their ridge, the ground sloped downward. Zandria saw it was not as steep as the walls near the entrance to the Dire Mines. She believed Tihi could easily make her way down into the immense valley that spread out before them. From their peak, she could see across all of it. With Blackwood Forest at her back, she knew this had to be the northern tip of Castlewood Forest. To the far east, she could even see where the ground started back up and the narrow trees of Truewood took root.

Dew pointed south and said, "There it is. Castlewood Castle."

Zandria could only see countless trees dotted with wide glens. She thought there might have been a river cutting through the center of the valley. Beyond that, she could make out nothing. Again, Zandria was reminded of the advantage of having elven eyes.

"All we have to do is cross this valley," said Zandria, feeling relieved.

"I certainly hope the wood spirits are as eager to let us pass," said Tihi. Then she spurred herself down the slope with a "Heeyaa."

As Tihi galloped down the rocky terrain, none of them heard the sound approaching from the rear. The steady clank and jingle of frying pans and chains could only belong to one wagon. Raymond Shaydaway had found their trail.

The slope proved easy for Tihi and soon Zandria and her two friends were surrounded by the natural beauty of Castlewood Forest. They continued down into the valley at a leisurely gait. Now, Zandria's thoughts were consumed with wood spirits. She did not know what to expect, but Dew and Tihi made them seem unfriendly.

It did not take long to learn the truth.

Zandria watched the deep woods closely. Every once in a while, she thought she caught a glimpse of something moving. The movement always happened out of the corner of her eye. By the time she focused on the area, all she could see was a swaying branch or settling leaves. She knew this movement could have been caused by the gentle breeze that cooled her cheeks, but did not believe that was the case.

She started to feel disappointed that they were not meeting the spirits. In her mind, Zandria expected the wood spirits to be generous and wise. She hoped they would be something like the Prismata fairies she met back home.

Her hopes faded when she started hearing whispers carried on the breeze. "Get out. Turn back. This is not your place."

"Is that what I think it is?" asked Zandria.

"Wood spirits," said Dew. "Wait until they really get started."

Zandria did not want to wait for them to get started. She did not want to meet anymore unfriendly creatures. She wondered why it seemed there were so many unpleasant people in the Northern Wood.

Then there was a loud creaking sound. Suddenly a thick branch bent down in front of them like a massive arm blocking their path. Tihi stopped in her tracks. Before she could turn around, more branches twisted and bent to completely close them in a trap.

"Here we go," said Dew, partly under her breath.

The gentle breeze blew harder and whipped around them. It quickly became a cyclone, picking up leaves and branches. Zandria had seen wind funnels like this back in Banookanook. Every year, strong storms would move out across the ocean, marking the end of the big fishing season. Sometimes, the wind in these storms would be so strong that it would stir up these furious funnels. After being so close to that kind of power, this miniature version did not frighten her, much.

A dark shape appeared in the center of the cyclone. Through all of the flying debris, Zandria could not see what it was. With its size, she did not allow for the possibility that it might be Shaydaway. Then the wind died out and the being spiraled down to the ground, coming to a graceful stop on two tiny legs. It looked to be the biggest rabbit Zandria had ever seen. Wider than he was tall, silky-looking brown fur covered his fat body, seeming to barely balance on those skinny little legs. His floppy ears hung down past his shoulders, one behind and the other in his face. He brushed it back slowly with his right paw. As he moved his arm back, his ear slid across until it draped behind him with the other. Almost amusing, Zandria held her smile because of his stern expression.

"My name ith Bajuk and you are trethpathing," he said from behind two thick front teeth.

"You mean trespassing," said Dew, clearly mocking his exaggerated speech.

"That's not possible," said Zandria. "This forest belongs to the Queen of the Northern Wood."

Bajuk responded, "Ha. Theethe woodth will never belong to a human. Ath protector of thith realm, I forbid you to travel any further."

The more the strange rabbit-like creature talked, the more Zandria wanted to laugh. It took every effort to keep a straight face in front of this less than frightening guardian. She said, "You don't understand. We have to get to Castlewood Castle."

"It ith you who doth not underthand. All thitithens of that plathe know thith valley ith thacred. You thall not path."

"Alright," said Dew. "That's enough. You can drop your act. Her sister is the Queen of the Eastern Sky and we're on an official errand."

"Why didn't you thay tho." Bajuk stuck both paws into his mouth and peeled his face back up over his head. The skin hung like a hood. Underneath, a nearly human head relieved Zandria from her imagination of the skull that might have greeted her. Zandria thought the beard and short hair covering the white face looked like fresh, green grass. "I really do enjoy dressing up in these costumes," Bajuk finished with a smile.

Zandria followed Dew's example and tried to act tough. "We don't have time for games. Shaydaway's carnival is probably following us right now." She did not think this was true, but wanted to sound urgent.

She was a little surprised when the cheerfulness ran out of his face. He said, "That man causes much trouble. I've lost too many friends to his carnival."

Bajuk looked around, then waved up into the tree tops. A strong gust of wind rushed down. He closed his eyes as it hit him in the face, waving the rabbit hood behind him. The breeze sailed past and Zandria could see it winding through the trees almost like it was a living creature. It disappeared somewhere behind them.

"They'll be watching for him now," said Bajuk.

"Who?" asked Zandria.

"Oh, I told the wood spirits that the carnival man may be in our forest."

"But I thought you were a wood spirit?" she said.

Bajuk looked embarrassed. "Not quite. It's complicated, but think of me as a spirit in training. I'm basically on guard duty until I earn my place. Don't worry about that now. You have to go."

Zandria said, "Thank you Bajuk. I hope you get to be a spirit soon."

"Thank you, my lady. Now head south. Take my shortcut across the dale by the river. In no time, you'll be heading into the human village." Bajuk pulled his rabbit mask back on and, as suddenly as he appeared, he disappeared in another small cyclone.

Tihi did not wait for any instructions from her riders and started to gallop. As Bajuk said, they entered the dale. To the right of the wide clearing, a huge river rushed by them back toward

Blackwood Forest. On the far side, in front of them, Zandria could see more trees, but beyond that, she thought she could make out rooftops and the faint outline of Castlewood Castle.

"That river comes from the spring in the castle cellars. The castle and woodsman's village get all their water from it," explained Dew.

"I didn't remember seeing a village when I was at Castlewood," said Zandria, honestly knowing she did not.

"It's on the north side of the castle. You were traveling east. It's only the home to all of the humans in the Northern Wood. I could see how you missed it," said Dew.

Zandria did not think she would ever get used to Dew's sarcasm. She rolled her eyes and tried to laugh about it. In the sky, she noticed a bird circling high above them. At first, she thought it might be another of Shaydaway's evil creatures. Then she recognized the type of bird.

"That's strange," she said.

Dew looked up, following her gaze. The bird sailed out of sight. "I've never seen a bird like it," she said.

"I have," Zandria said. "Back home, back in Banookanook. They live by the ocean. But that's not the strange part. I could have sworn it was gold."

The sight of the seagull, gold or otherwise, awoke a hundred memories in Zandria. Suddenly, for the first time since she left Banookanook, she felt homesick. The panic of leaving and the excitement of everything that followed pushed the small village by the sea out of her head. Then after the Rockhorn Battle, she explored Castle Empyrean and found her mother's crystal. She simply had not had time to be homesick before now.

As they raced across the open field, Zandria's mind raced over the Dead Forest and through the jungle. She tried hard to picture Banookanook. She tried to picture her home and the other huts made from giant seashells. However, the image of the crashing waves filled her head. Only vague suggestions of the rest of Banookanook came to her. Even though she lived there for ten years, she could not remember the face of a single one of her neighbors.

The idea of something so important to her vanishing so easily made her sad. If Dew noticed the tears sneaking out of the corners of her eyes, she would say the wind in her face caused it. She had never been homesick before and never knew it could feel so bad. Still, her heart glowed. She felt this warmth start in Empyrean's bell chamber, but now she wished it would not drown out this one feeling. She wanted to hold on to her past. She feared if she let it go, she would lose the memories of both her mother and father that were already fading.

Before she could think any more about it, a low rumbling came from behind them. It was accompanied by an eerily familiar jingling of metal. Tihi stopped to look. Zandria and Dew turned around, too. The rumbling came from

Shaydaway's wagon wheels tearing across the ground and the jingling from the donkey's chains.

Zandria could not believe how fast they were going. She could not believe the donkey could survive that pace. She could also not believe the wagon wheels would not splinter and break. Yet here he came, directly toward them.

Tihi turned to flee, but Shaydaway's magician Lazarou suddenly blocked their path. He waved one arm and let loose a sparkly powder. The sparkles danced and shimmered in the sunlight as they fell around her. Zandria barely inhaled any of it and instantly fell asleep. She had a vague idea that Dew and Tihi came quickly behind her.

When she finally awoke late in the evening, Zandria found them surrounded by the Carnival Chaotica's star performers, illuminated by a blazing campfire. Lazarou with his ashy, black skin stood in front of her. The strongman, Gaunt, held Tihi's reins although she lay on the ground still asleep. The horrific skeleton man called MacBeth must be watching Dew on the other side, she guessed. She knew Dew was on the ground behind her. She could feel they were tied back to back and was disappointed that this should be a feeling easy for her to recognize. Then she saw the misfigured dwarf, Saman, scampering toward the wagon, which must have held Mister Shaydaway.

He repeated, "She's avake. She's avake," as he climbed up to knock on the wagon door.

After a moment, Raymond Shaydaway made his entrance. He wore the same white suit, still in pristine condition. As he stepped through the doorway, he put on his tall, skinny ringleader's top hat. He looked deliberate as he walked toward her in silence.

Stopping less than an arm's reach away, he said, "You have something that I want." He paused, looking to be lost in thought, then leaning in close, he said, "Forgive me. Something that I *need*."

His foul breath stung Zandria's nostrils. She answered defiantly, "Sorry, I'm all out of breath freshener."

"Blast you, child." Now Shaydaway looked exasperated. "The crystals. I'm talking about the crystals. You have them and don't even know how to use them."

"What crystals," said Zandria.

"We don't have any crystals," added Dew. Zandria felt some relief with her elven friend now awake.

Shaydaway looked on the verge of losing his calm. Zandria did not know if this would help their situation or make the man more dangerous.

He leaned in close and said, "Give me the Trammeler. The four crystals. I can't take them from you. That's not how it works. If it did, you'd already be dead. You have to give them to me willingly."

Zandria realized that he did not know how many crystals she had. She did not know if this secret could be used to her advantage, but it did make her feel a little safer. When he stood up away from her, she could feel Dew wriggling behind her, like she had been waiting for him to move. Then she instantly freed their wrists from the binding ropes.

Saman pointed at the partially unbound girls with his hoof-hand as he jumped up and down with excitement.

"It doesn't matter," said Shaydaway. "Where are they going to go without their horse? Mr. Gaunt is not likely to be outmatched by a saddle sore mare."

"Friesians don't get saddle sore," exclaimed a new voice.

Zandria looked around to see who spoke. A Friesian stallion charged out of the darkness. He knocked back Lazarou and MacBeth before they could react.

Tihi jumped up wide-awake from the commotion and tried to pull away from Gaunt. His grip seemed too strong for her. Then, out of the night, a man with skin like iron, stepped up behind the carnival strongman. She thought Gaunt was tall, but this new, iron behemoth stood at least a foot taller than the strongman. With one flat open palm, the iron man slapped Gaunt on the chest. Gaunt stumbled back, letting go of Tihi.

While she watched the turmoil around her, Zandria barely noticed the hands loosening the last of her ropes. She turned around, expecting to see Dew, but she knelt face to face with Adam.

"Now would be a good time to go," he said. He called to his Friesian companion, "Kalis, over here."

Kalis came quickly and Adam mounted equally as quick. He offered a hand to Zandria. She looked back to see Dew safely mounting Tihi. The elf nodded to her across the campfire, so Zandria took Adam's hand.

"Eisenhahn, we're leaving," shouted Adam.

Eisenhahn stopped trying to swat Saman from scurrying around his legs and followed them. Even amid this nightmare, Zandria had to smile at the size difference between the pesky dwarf and the amazing man with iron skin.

The friends raced away, leaving the Carnival Chaotica in chaos.

Chapter 16

The Trip to the Great Cliffs

William raced through the Dead Forest. He could not believe he was actually thankful for his continually smaller size. It made it easier to dodge the brambles. He could duck between trees and under low branches without slowing down. He hoped this advantage would help him catch up to Vanril. The he realized the dwarf would have the same advantage.

He felt bad about leaving Aleta with the injured Smoltz and Terg's body. However, they only had two horses left. William knew he could trust the Friesians to help her.

Before he left, he heard Sulis say, "I would be honored to carry the fallen soldier."

Aleta shared the other saddle with the last and youngest of the Smoltz Brothers. His injury was severe enough that he needed someone to help him. Otherwise, Aleta said she wanted to go after Vanril with William. He had to insist she go back to Castle Empyrean or he believed Smoltz would never make it.

"If I do not stop Vanril, then you must return and bring our army down on top of him."

"You are no more than a boy now. How can you stop him?" said Aleta. He saw concern on her normally stoic face for the first time since he had known her.

"I have my mind and my skill," said William. "Besides, I'm still bigger than he is."

William helped Aleta secure Terg's body on Sulis. Then he put some food in a small pouch for himself and double-checked the sharpness of his new knife. He watched Aleta mount the other Friesian helping Smoltz stay in the saddle. They rode off to the west. He knew from here, with luck, they could be at Castle Empyrean in only a few days.

William followed Vanril's tracks almost in a straight line toward the town of Bremen. He had no idea where Adam was and he left Hum and Reinholdt safe in Bond. Now with the others heading back to Empyrean, he was on his own. This did not feel like the same solitude as when he first awoke from the ice. Although his world changed, he had someone in it now. He had a family. So even though he was without companions, for the first time he did not *feel* alone.

This thought renewed his purpose and he pushed on without rest. Sometime in the middle of the night, he made it to the town of Bremen.

Even in the dark, he could see how different it was. The animals dedicated themselves to improving the town and making it a sanctuary. The streets were clean and buildings were repaired, at least, as good as animals could repair them.

He crossed the main intersection of the town and saw no sign of any animals or, to his relief, the sky rock that poisoned and hypnotized them not too long ago. He recognized the building where he was held prisoner with Zandria and Olena. It looked empty now. On the opposite corner, a hound dog slept in front of the door like a guard.

William stepped past the dog without disturbing him and knocked on the door. He did not know if he would find who he was looking for inside, but he had to start somewhere. The hound dog did not wake at the knocking sound either. Good guard, thought William. After a moment, the door opened from inside and an enormous white tiger poked out his head. William guessed the right door.

"Who's there?" he growled, looking over the top of William's head, due to his large size.

"Virgata, it's me, Prince William." The soft voice saying his own name sounded strange in his young ears.

Virgata, mayor of Bremen and friend of humans, lowered his striped head.

"You smell like my friend, but you do not look like him," said the tiger.

William could not resist wrapping his arms around Virgata's thick furry neck. He hugged him like a child hugging a beloved pet. Where did this strange urge come from, he asked himself. With the growing memory loss and these childish urges, he knew he did not have long to fulfill his promise. At this rate, he feared it would not be too many days before he turned into a baby. Then what came next, he wondered.

The tiger broke his thoughts by shaking him loose. The guard dog momentarily growled in his sleep, shifted his weight and draped a paw over his face. It amused William to see him sleeping so soundly with a stranger on his doorstep.

"Come in," said Virgata. "Tell me what brings you to our town at such an hour. Let me say, I do have a guess what it involves."

Virgata stretched out on the floor and William sat crossed legged in front of him in the moonlit room. The boy recounted the events that occurred since his rescue party last passed through Bremen. He left out the part about Adam being related to him. Other than Aleta, who helped him find the truth, he wanted Adam to be the first to know.

When William finished telling of Vanril's atrocities, Virgata said, "I suspected as much. Now sleep. In the morning, I will provide you with some missing information. There is nothing more that can be done tonight, especially in your state."

William agreed, finding himself drifting off as he watched Virgata's tail dance back and forth.

He slept on the floor next to the tiger and awoke with the sun. He did not look forward to confronting Vanril because he did not know if he could count on his changing body. Still, he knew it had to be done and wanted to start as soon as possible.

Despite his magnificence, Virgata did not seem to like being awake this early. He licked his paw repeatedly and rubbed it over his left ear. William wondered if this was normal morning grooming or a way to soothe a headache.

"I will have my best trackers set you on your course," said Virgata. "Before you go, I told you I have some information for you. The day after you left us to save the children, a pack of dwarves came through our town. They were attempting to recruit us to their cause. As you can guess, they found none sympathetic to their words. Many of my brothers and sisters are still recuperating from wounds caused by those same dwarves and their rock monsters."

"He had a few Rockhorn with him and some werewolves. But, I think he is alone now," William added.

Virgata continued, "All the better. One of the serpents told me he revealed his true cause. He is searching for a sacred site that holds the answer to restoring these tormented lands."

"I knew it," said William.

The white tiger stretched his paws out in front of him as far as they would go. Then he raised his hind legs to stretch his back with his long tail pointing straight up. William heard the big feline's back crack a couple times.

"Don't think he means to repent. He is looking to destroy whatever it is. My only relief is that I do not think he has found its hiding place. However, there are only a few sacred places in the East," said Virgata.

William pondered this for a moment, saddened by how much things had changed. In his time, Soria Moria was the only sacred place. "Besides the ancient castle, where else?"

"There is a place covered in ice that used to be a town called Frostwick. I've never met a human that would dare venture there."

"I don't think that's it," said William knowingly. It made him feel a little special that his long time resting place was considered sacred these days.

"There is one other possibility. Far to the south, beyond the unicorn meadow, there is a waterfall where the Chromisarc River meets the Great Cliffs," said Virgata.

William jumped up with excitement. He knew that place. In fact, he crossed that very river the day they had their second fatal encounter with Vanril. More importantly, he knew the waterfall from Zandria's stories.

"The Prismata," he said.

"I do not know that name," said the tiger. "However, I have heard it to be the hiding place of the Rainbow Princesses, a flock of sisters rumored to be quite powerful."

"I think they are one and the same."

After their conversation, they breakfasted on fruit and fresh milk courtesy of a mother goat. Then, Virgata instructed several canines and birds to sniff out Vanril's trail. It did not take long for them to find it.

With preparations made, William left Bremen. Virgata offered some animal assistance, but William feared they would only slow him down. He knew time was crucial now.

"What happens if you become too young to stop the dwarf?" asked Virgata.

"If I don't stop Vanril, then it won't matter what happens to me."

The knowledge of the possibility of saving the Royal Forest pushed him. William crossed the wasteland faster this time than any before. He entered the strange mix of jungle and what was left of the Royal Forest before sunrise.

At the first hint of light, he glimpsed something moving ahead of him. Whatever it was, it stood no taller than him. The top of it did not even stick out of the underbrush. William gained on it as quickly as he could through the tangles of vines and thick tree roots.

The creature led him to an opening in the jungle. In the center of the clearing, he saw a perfectly still pool. The water in the pool came from a thundering waterfall on the far side that spilled off the Great Cliffs. William could not believe that the lagoon did not even ripple under the thousands of gallons of crashing water. He suspected this was truly a sacred and magical place.

Then William looked for the creature he had been following. Now, in the open, he could see it was Vanril. He watched the dwarf heading toward a cave behind the waterfall.

"Vanril," he shouted. He did not think his high, childish voice sounded very threatening.

Vanril looked back and changed directions for the cliff. He gripped the damp rock with his pudgy hands and started climbing. William did not hesitate to go after him. Soon, they were both scaling the slippery wall. The dwarf managed to stay a few feet above the boy as they went, but at least William kept him from the cave.

As they climbed, William did not think of the height. He did not think of the rushing water to his right. He did not think of the loose rocks Vanril kept dropping at him. All he could think about was saving the Royal Forest, his forest. He did not know how to do it, but he knew stopping Vanril was the first step. He could not allow the evil dwarf to destroy his only chance of returning some beauty to his land.

His small hands and feet moved automatically up the cliff. Then, it happened. His little body betrayed him. He guessed he was no more than five years old and a five year old did not have the dexterity he needed right now. When William reached for the next outcropping, his arm was too short. He missed and almost fell a hundred feet. The small boy dangled by one hand, realizing how high up he actually was.

Above him, Vanril kept going. For a stocky little person, William thought he was surprisingly agile. Then Vanril came to a ledge where he could not reach the next higher level. Due to the shape of the rocks, the only way he could go was toward the waterfall.

William took this chance to catch him. He regained his footing and pulled himself up to the ledge. Vanril stopped moving, apparently afraid to challenge the madly pouring water. He pulled a dagger out of his belt and swung it at William. William leaned back, almost losing his balance, to avoid the knife. Then he grabbed his own knife and attacked Vanril.

They battled on that ledge for a time that felt much longer than it actually was. Barely audible over the waterfall, their short knives clinked with each stroke. In a deft move, Vanril twisted his arm and knocked William's knife from his hand. The blade flashed, reflecting sunlight as it twirled its way to the bottom.

This angered William. With an unaffected body, he would have defeated Vanril in an instant, even hanging from this cliff. Now, he balanced himself, with no weapon, waiting for Vanril to finish the fight.

The dwarf struck at William's secure hand, trying to knock him off the wall. William did not care about his own life at this point. It outraged him that his failure would mean the end of the Royal Forest forever, as well as empty promises to Terg and Adam.

Vanril swung again. This time, William grabbed Vanril's wrist with his free hand. The dwarf, now several inches taller, stood over him.

He let go of the rock to push the knife with both hands. William could not hold him with one, so he had no choice but to grab him with both hands. Still, the knife tip came closer to his face.

"You're done boy," snarled Vanril.

"I won't let you win," was all William could say.

They struggled, somehow keeping their balance with only space for their toes on that ledge.

Then something strange happened.

Bright light flashed out of the cave way down below. The light separated into individual colors of red, orange, yellow, blue, green and violet. The rainbow spiraled and flashed upward, surrounding them.

"Let go," came a woman's soft voice.

Apparently, Vanril heard it too. He stopped pressing and looked down into the light. William did not think the voice was talking to Vanril. He had a guess that this was the Prismata and put his trust in them. He let go of Vanril and fell back off the cliff. Vanril leaned over to watch William fall and slipped off too.

The boy and dwarf tumbled through the air.

Chapter 17

Together Again

They rode all night.

Tihi and Kalis stayed neck and neck, matching each other's speed. Zandria kept looking over her shoulder, expecting Shaydaway to be right behind them.

He was not.

"Why do you keep looking back?" asked Adam, turning to make eye contact.

"They must be chasing us," said Zandria.

"Inconceivable," he said. "I loosened the wheel bolts on that cart when his back was turned."

Zandria squeezed Adam tightly. He rescued her and she knew then that she loved him. She was not in love with him. That concept was still many years beyond her. Besides, she thought, being married to a boy would be gross. Still, she loved him with the deep, warm encompassing love of a true friend. She rode the rest of the night with her arms around his middle and her head resting on his back.

As the morning sun rose in the west, Zandria saw Adam's copper hair for the first time.

She said, "I like your new look."

"This was an accident," he said, pushing his fingers through his hair.

"Well, it suits you," Zandria finished, genuinely liking the reflective look.

"Speaking of new looks, your bruise is almost gone," said Adam.

Zandria put her hand to her cheek. She had forgotten about hitting the door the night she found the first crystal. It seemed so long ago since that injury started this whole journey.

Then she turned her thoughts to the crystals. She saw the two tucked into the side of Adam's waistband. Like Olena predicted, they now had four of them. Then she wondered how Shaydaway knew about the crystals. He even had a name for them, the Trammeler. Maybe, like Dew said, he could sense magical items. But how could he know its name? Maybe he knew something more and was already looking for the crystals. Maybe he knew something about her mother.

Her thoughts were interrupted by the early morning sights and sounds as they approached the village. Now Zandria understood why she did not see it when she first came to Castlewood Castle.

Built on the slope of the valley, even the tallest house in the village remained hidden beneath the castle when looking north from the courtyard. Zandria settled on calling this place a village, because she did not know a word that meant something bigger. The houses and shops spread out around her much farther than Banookanook and probably even more than Edge Town and Bremen combined. She had never seen so many people living together in one place.

The horses slowed to a walk on the cobblestone streets. Apparently, they felt safe enough to move slower now. They entered the massive town square. In the center, a tall fountain decorated with fish and bird statues bubbled cheerfully. Zandria saw one of the statues on top looked out of place. All of the other carvings were stone and this one was gold. When she saw the seagull dip to drink the gurgling water, she knew it was the same one she saw circling them yesterday.

Adam shouted, "Good morning, Crumb."

The seagull spotted Adam and swooped down to perch on his extended forearm.

"This is Crumb," Adam said to Zandria. "He found you for me."

"And that's Eisenhahn," Zandria remembered his name from last night. She saw the iron man looking at dolls and puppets for sale in front of a wood carver's shop. She added, "My friends are Dew Lantisphere and..."

"The Silent Tihi," interrupted Kalis, apparently demonstrating his superiority over the female of his species.

Zandria almost forgot. Tihi did not speak in front of the other Friesians. She worried that it would be harder to keep her secret now being used to hearing her voice. She did not think Dew would have the same problem. Elves seemed to be naturally secretive. Luckily, Kalis inadvertently reminded her not to give away Tihi's secret.

Then the smell of baking bread reminded her that she was starving. She watched a fruit seller busy herself setting up her cart for the day. Dew hopped down from Tihi. With some friendly conversation, she secured some breakfast for them all.

The group sat on some benches in one corner of the market, eating their fruits and pastries. Zandria found herself relaxing for a moment. She did feel safer, surrounded by people in the daylight, especially with Adam. She could not imagine Shaydaway or any of his carnival people trying to confront them here. Besides, they would soon be in the safety of Castlewood Castle. From there, she planned, a squad of soldiers could escort them back to Castle Empyrean.

Adam spoke between bites, "What do you call this place?"

"The market," said Dew. She gave Adam a look like she thought he was stupid. Zandria guessed this to be the same look she would give any male.

"Thanks, but I meant this whole town," Adam said without seeming offended. "What is the name of this town?"

Dew said, "It's not a town, it's a village. And it's called Lochnoble."

Before they left, the market gradually became crowded with hundreds of Lochnobilians, all starting their day. People started trading their goods. Children carrying books marched off to a place Dew called school.

"School sounds horrible," said Adam, making a disgusted face.

"It couldn't be worse than being a slave in a mine," said Zandria.

"You don't know that," he retorted with a smile. "You spent your whole life on a beach."

They left Lochnoble feeling welcome and in good spirits. Everyone they passed from the market to the castle greeted them like old friends. Recognized by a few people, Dew stopped a couple times for short conversations. Everybody's good mood almost made Zandria forget about Shaydaway.

They crested the last short hill and crossed the wide courtyard that Zandria recognized from her previous visit. As they entered the open castle gates, she saw a poster hung on the heavy wooden door. Zandria froze in her tracks, overwhelmed by dread.

"What's it say, Zan?" asked Adam, standing by her side.

She could not bring herself to answer.

Then Eisenhahn said, "I like the picture. It looks like a circus."

"It's not," said Dew. "It says, the Carnivale Chaotica and Pandemonium Sideshow is coming your way soon."

"That's the guy, isn't it?" asked Adam, pointing at the figure in the center of the poster.

"That's him," said Zandria with a shiver.

Professor Erbadin met them at the gate. Referring to the poster, he said, "Sounds fun.

Someone posted that sign this morning. Didn't see who, but it wasn't that long ago. They're probably still close." Erbadin waved his short arms, "Well, come on in."

Shocked, Zandria mumbled, "How could he beat us here?"

Adam had to pull her by the arm to get her into the castle courtyard. He addressed the dwarf, "Sir, I have some important matters to discuss. First, we need some rest and it would do the queen's sister some comfort if you would lock your castle gates."

Professor Erbadin stopped walking. "Lock the castle keep? These doors have not even been shut since, well, since the Vanril incident. That's been a hundred years."

Dew spoke, "We were accosted last night in the valley."

"Wood spirits," said the dwarf like he had to spit out the word.

"No, by them," Dew said, pointing at the poster.

"It's true," added Kalis.

Looking confused, Professor Erbadin said, "I'll close them out of respect for the new queen. For the record, I am not scared of traveling entertainers."

He gestured to the gate guard and the man closed the door once Zandria's entire group came inside.

A stablehand led Tihi and Kalis to the stables and Crumb followed them, probably searching for food, Zandria guessed. Eisenhahn asked to stay outside. He said, "I don't like to go into small places. They are too small." Zandria already thought of him as a big child and instantly liked him.

Professor Erbadin personally showed the rest of them to the same bedroom Zandria used six nights ago. Dew fell asleep before the dwarf left the room. Adam offered to sleep on the floor, so Zandria shared the bed with Dew. Before lying down, Adam handed his two crystals to her.

He said, "I hope this helps your mother."

"Thank you," said Zandria. Holding all four crystals gave her a sense of accomplishment matched only by her weariness. She did not know what to do with the crystals yet, but even if she did, she knew now was not the time. She needed to be sure the crystals were safe from Shaydaway first.

Sleep came heavy and dreamless, but it did not seem to last long enough. Zandria still felt exhausted when she awoke to Adam shouting. She roused Dew and then followed the sound of his voice outside. She came out in time to see him racing across the courtyard.

"Do not open that gate!" he yelled.

A dwarf and two men stopped at Adam's command. Then Professor Erbadin came up behind Zandria. Dew followed quickly behind him.

"That boy needs to relax," said Erbadin.

"Raymond Shaydaway is a bad man. If you let him in here, he'll take these." Zandria held up the four crystals. She noticed they glowed slightly even in the sunlight now that they were all together.

"You have the Trammeler? I knew you were on no vacation," exclaimed Erbadin.

"I thought nobody knew about these crystals," Dew said to Zandria.

"Snow White...I mean, Her Majesty confided in me five or six years ago. She asked me never to mention it, but I did not expect it truly existed. I couldn't believe in anything that could ensnare one of the queens."

"So, it is a prison," said Zandria, determined to be right. "How do I open it?"

"I don't know how it works. I didn't even know it was real until a moment ago. Right now, we have more pressing concerns if this carnival man is after it," said Professor Erbadin.

He rushed off to command the defense of Castlewood Castle. By that time, Adam climbed the steps on the outside wall. Zandria wanted to figure out how the crystals worked, but she knew the time for that was after they stopped Shaydaway. She found a dusty leather pouch among some saddle equipment and tucked the crystals safely inside it. She slung the pouch across her back and joined Adam and Dew on the high wall.

When she looked down, she could not see Raymond Shaydaway. However, Saman led the poor donkey away from the castle, so that the wagon blocked their only escape on the North Road.

As soon as the wagon stopped moving, the back door popped open. Lazarou, Gaunt and MacBeth came out first. They were immediately followed by twenty interlopers. Zandria had seen the inside of the wagon and knew that so many people could not fit inside such a small space. Shaydaway definitely had some magic. To her surprise, ten more figures came out of the wagon after the interlopers.

These new men were like none Zandria had ever seen. They wore dull, baggy clothes with too many pockets and odd shaped patches. Most of them had bushy, curly hair, but all of them looked like they had never washed it. Some wore oversized gloves and a few had shoes that looked twice the size of their feet. However, each one had makeup on his face. They did not have the beautiful look of the queens'. Their makeup looked old and smudged, like they did not care how it went on or how it looked. They did not use bright, happy colors either. Mostly, they painted their faces with blacks, reds and browns.

Dew said, "Clowns. Why did it have to be clowns? I hate clowns."

Zandria did not know what a clown was, but, so far, she saw no reason to like them either.

The myriad of carnival workers stood in silence.

Then a gust of wind whipped through the woods, strong enough to blow the poster from the wooden gate. The advertisement curled through the air and landed on its back. Zandria watched in amazement as the painted picture of Shaydaway began to move as if he were walking closer to the front of the poster. An instant later, his arm poked out, ripping through the paper. He immediately stuck his other hand through, found purchase on the ground surrounding the poster and pulled himself out of it.

Zandria first thought he came out of the ground, but the paper slipped away when he pulled his last foot loose. She saw no hole underneath. She could only imagine that he actually was in the picture. She guessed he could pass from one poster to another wherever his minions hung them. What a terrible power, she thought to herself, nowhere would be safe.

Shaydaway stood in the middle of the courtyard with his hands on his hips, almost glistening in his pristine suit. He spoke and his voice echoed off the high stone walls. "My dear, sweet child, you must give me the Trammeler willingly. I will eliminate every person in your little fortress until only you are left. When you are all alone, you will have no choice."

Then, the magician Lazarou raised his right arm into the air. His hand burst into flame and he pointed it at the castle. A huge fireball shot toward the gate. Zandria expected them to be through in moments, but the flames died out instantly.

"Vexwood," said Professor Erbadin triumphantly. Zandria did not notice he joined them on the wall. He climbed up on a box to look down at the attackers.

He continued, "Our alchemists found a fireproof tree in Vexwood Forest. Strangest thing. They coated the gate with its bark. I want to finish Castle Empyrean's bridge with it." Then he yelled to Shaydaway, "You have until the count of three to leave here and forget about this child."

Shaydaway said nothing, but smiled his thin sinister smile.

"One," said Erbadin.

Northern soldiers quickly lined the wall and readied their bows.

Raymond Shaydaway bowed. For a moment, Zandria hoped he was preparing to leave. Then Shaydaway nodded to Mr. Gaunt.

"Two," said the old dwarf.

The northern soldiers took aim.

The enormous strongman, Mr. Gaunt, walked up to the gate. He flexed his muscles and clasped his hands together. He swung his double fist hard against the door. Zandria heard the thick wood crack from her high spot on the wall.

Before Gaunt pounded again, Professor Erbadin shouted, "Three!"

At the same time Mr. Gaunt smashed the first hole in the gate, the soldiers fired their arrows. The interlopers hit by arrows disappeared in flashes of light. Even during the battle, Zandria hoped they were freed and sent back to their own worlds. The clowns, however, proved to be more acrobatic. No soldier could hit a single clown. The scary-faced men tumbled and rolled clear of every shot.

Mr. Gaunt almost made it through the gate, but he was knocked back in a shower of splinters. Without being told, Eisenhahn joined the fight, smashing out of the gate to meet the enemy. When he came near to Shaydaway, the thin man dashed for the safety of his wagon, pushing Saman off the steps.

Eisenhahn stood over the bewildered Gaunt. Zandria could not hear what Eisenhahn said to the stunned man lying on his back, but then Gaunt kicked him in the stomach. As the two giants brawled, clowns and interlopers poured through the open gate.

"Is this what you wanted to discuss?" Erbadin asked Adam.

"I tried to warn you," Adam said.

"If it makes you feel better, I now have reason to be scared of entertainers. Take these two ladies to safety," said Professor Erbadin. "There is a secret passage through the fireplace in your bedroom." Then he grabbed his axe and leapt from the wall into the courtyard. Zandria saw him last clinging to a clown's back.

She followed Adam and Dew, winding through the fight into the castle. It seemed extremely quiet indoors compared to the din of the battle. They moved cautiously down the empty hallway. When they came to the end of the hall, Adam could not decide to turn left or right.

"Which way?" he asked.

"This way," Zandria and Dew said at the same time, each pointing in different directions.

"Wait here," Adam said. He dashed to the left, looking for the correct room.

While they waited in silence, Zandria heard a faint jingle somewhere behind them. She turned around and peered down the dim hall, fearing what might have made that noise.

"What?" asked Dew.

Zandria hushed her. The noise came again. This time, Dew's face lit up with recognition. Zandria heard the jingle again, closer. Then she heard the solid boom of a big drum. Zandria knew her fear came true. MacBeth, the carnival musician, was coming. Because his twisted skeleton made its own noise, he had little chance of sneaking up on them. Now the thump and clink came at a fast tempo.

MacBeth appeared from around the corner at the far end of the hall. He stood there waiting and then blew a horrible screeching noise through the hole in his chin that sounded anything but musical. He slammed both bulging elbows against the stretched skin of his curved back and charged, flashing between the light and shadow of the high windows as he came.

Ching.

The metal piercings rattled on his arms.

Boom.

His elbows pounded a rhythm on his back skin.

Ching.

He came fast.

Boom.

Adam grabbed Zandria's shoulder from behind. She screamed and then he screamed in response. Then Macbeth stopped next to them. He blew another note through his chin hole that sounded like a scream.

Adam lunged, jabbing his short sword into that gaping hole. The tip poked out through the top of MacBeth's head. The contorted man tried to blow again, but only air whistled out. Then he fell to the ground with one final strike on his drum.

"It's the other way," said Adam. He did not bother retrieving his sword, but instead pulled each girl by the hand.

They found the bedroom and all three climbed into the empty fireplace without hesitation. Not knowing what to look for, Zandria watched Adam push on the back wall until it open onto a dark tunnel. Remembering the Taenarum Tunnel at Soria Moria, she wondered if dark tunnels were the preferred way to get to places outside of Banookanook. She felt like she had been through enough tunnels and mines already. This tunnel quickly covered her in ash and soot as soon as she crawled into it.

Dew crawled in last, but before she was safe, two of the terrible clowns grabbed her ankles.

"Go," she shouted as the clowns pulled her back into the room. She struggled futilely to get free.

"No," cried Zandria, reaching for her.

The secret door fell closed when Dew was pulled back into the fireplace. Adam quickly locked it from the inside. Then he dragged Zandria with him down the tunnel.

The escape tunnel opened into the forest amid a cluster of large rocks. Crumb the seagull sat waiting for them on the biggest rock.

"You made it." Adam sounded glad to see the golden bird. He added, "What about Eisenhahn?"

Crumb blinked once, but made no other movement or sound.

"We have to go back. We have to help Dew," cried Zandria.

"We can't go back. There's nothing we can do right now," said Adam. He put his arm around her shoulders and they started to follow Crumb away from the castle. Zandria reluctantly followed, mostly in shock and not sure what to do.

Zandria could still hear the sounds of fighting, but the battle did not reach this far. Then she heard another sound. A steady thump-thump came towards them. The sound frightened Crumb away. Zandria did not want to see MacBeth chasing them with a sword sticking out of his head. To her relief, Tihi appeared around the bend, her hoofs beating the ground like a drum.

"Get on," she said.

Adam said, "You can talk?"

"All Friesians can talk. Very few are smart enough to know when to close their mouth. Now get on."

Adam helped Zandria up first. Then he climbed onto Tihi's bareback behind her.

"Where are we going?" asked Zandria as they rode away from Castlewood Castle.

Tihi said, "Peckwood Forest."

Chapter 18

Eisenhahn's Ballad

Things did not stay in Eisenhahn's head very long. That really did not bother him. He did not mind his iron skin either. He never got hot or cold, but it itched sometimes. He liked his life, but some days he forgot his own name.

The day he met the boy was one of those days.

His only task was tending the path for a master whose face he could not remember.

He did remember his master's name. He called him Wizard Lumpkin because he was never allowed to call the old man by his first name, Karl.

Most days, he could not remember that name either.

Now, he had a new task, tending after this boy.

He tried to remember the boy's name, but all he could remember was his funny copper hair.

Somehow, the boy knew his name and that helped him remember.

"Eisenhahn," he told himself every night before falling asleep.

Now, he knew he had to protect this boy. So, they took a long walk. Along the way, he had to save the boy from ice and fire.

Then little black creatures tried to get in his mouth. He squished as many of them as he could until the creatures ran away into the forest.

This boy took him to many new places.

In this new place, Eisenhahn met a man that was almost as big as him. The man wanted to hurt the boy's friend, so he had to stop him.

That night, he said to himself, "I think that mean man is stronger than me. What's my name?"

Now he was at a castle and the strong man came back. The strong man tried to break down the door, but he stopped him.

Then he remembered, "My name is Eisenhahn."

"What?" said the strong man and then kicked him in the stomach.

Eisenhahn did not like that.

They stood in front of the castle, fighting each other.

With each punch, Eisenhahn said, "My name is Eisenhahn."

The strong man hit back. "Stop saying that," he yelled.

Finally, the strong man did not fight anymore. He lay on the ground, without moving. He thought the man might be asleep. Eisenhahn hit the man a few more times to make sure he stayed asleep.

"My name is Eisenhahn. I will... not... forget... that."

The other scary strangers ran away, but he could not find the boy anywhere. He decided to stay at the castle because it was safe now.

Then he remembered, "Adam. That's his name. I hope Adam is safe."

Chapter 19

William Finds an Answer

As he fell, William could feel himself slowing. He watched Vanril fall after him and then drop past him. He rolled over, air rushing against his face. He could see the dwarf getting further away and knew he was falling faster than himself. The bright colors held him and it felt wonderful.

Magic, he thought. He loved the way it felt. It reminded him of the old days.

Then the flowing waterfall stopped. It did not slow to a trickle, it simply stopped. The rapidly approaching lagoon dried up instantly as well.

From this height, he could barely make out Vanril slap against the muddy bottom. He knew no one could survive something like that. Then he realized he was quickly approaching the same fate. He did not think, even with the rainbow slowing him, that he could survive this landing unscathed.

As quickly as the waterfall stopped, after Vanril hit the bottom, it turned on again. William splashed into a full lagoon. Then he blacked out.

When William woke up, he found himself snuggled in a warm pile of blankets and pillows. He never imagined it could feel so good on his naked skin. Why was he naked, he wondered? He tried to look at his body, but could not lift his head. He could feel his arms moving, so he knew he was not restrained like a prisoner.

Then he saw his hands waving in front of his face. Except, they were not his hands, they were the hands of a baby. He did not want to believe they were his because he could not control their movement. He concentrated and felt his legs kicking in the same uncontrollable way.

He imagined the shock of this dawning realization to be greater than it was. While unconscious, he turned into a baby.

"Help me," he heard in his head, but what came out of his mouth sounded like "Ga gagga."

It was a strange sensation having the mind of a man in a baby's body, but he could feel that slipping away as well. Everything started to collapse in on itself. People and things he knew disappeared from his memory. Words that made sense only a few minutes ago were now gibberish. Even sensations, like his bare skin against the blankets, felt new and startling.

William held on to one last thought. He wanted to tell Adam that they were family before he came to whatever end was coming. The last word that he heard in his head was *Adam*, but he no longer knew what it meant.

"A-da," he heard himself say.

Then something appeared at the edge of his unfocusing vision. The shape moved back and forth in a very comforting motion. William tried to form a thought as to who or what it could be. Nothing came into his head.

"Rest, sweet William," said the shape. The words came to his tiny ears and they made sense. For a moment, his body stopped changing. He felt on the verge of becoming nothing, then, suddenly, he could feel his mind reinforcing itself.

Everything did not come back all at once. At first, only simple things happened, like being able to grab the blanket and see more in focus.

He looked at the shape hovering over him.

"Ma-ma," he said automatically.

William thought he saw his mother. She looked down at him and smiled. He knew it could not be her. She had been gone for more than five hundred years.

Still, the woman seemed familiar.

He started to remember Adam and wondered if it could be Adam's mother. As his eyesight cleared, he recognized the woman from somewhere else.

William now had a faint memory of standing next to the boy named Adam. The boy held something in his hand, something powerful. In it, he saw a beautiful woman. Could this be Zandria's mother, he asked himself. Then, he asked himself, who is Zandria? After that, things returned quickly with his mind in overdrive, rebuilding itself.

He remembered Zandria and Olena. He remembered Fury, the dragon Evorin, and the Rockhorn Battle. He remembered discovering he was Adam's uncle, a few generations removed. This made him happy and made him feel like he belonged in this world. He hoped Adam would feel the same. Then he remembered this woman standing over him, *his* lost queen.

She looked down on him with simple, pure beauty. This was his queen, his one true love. She looked as young and vibrant as the day she left for Soria Moria. He did not see her with the age and changes of five hundred years, like she looked the day a wretched beast in service of the Forgotten Evil took her forever.

"William," she said.

"I am here," he answered in baby talk. He knew she could understand him, though.

"William, so short is the precious gift of time. It is not to be wasted," she said. "Only a rare few have the opportunity to start over."

He stared at her in awe. It had been so long and his heart ached at the sight of her. She slipped in and out of focus as his body adjusted itself. He wanted to hold her, to tell her he still loved her after all this time.

She continued, "There are others that need you now. I can give you the gift of starting over so you can help them. But, you must give up your memories of me. You cannot live in two different worlds or two different times. I can erase five hundred years and give you a normal life in this time."

William did not hesitate. He got what he wanted. He got to see her one last time, to tell her he loved her, if only in his head and through the goo's and gah's of baby gibberish. He knew he had a duty and friends and family that needed him here and now. He said "Yes", but it came out sounding like, "Ya-ga."

William blinked his eyes and she was gone. He blinked again and his twenty-five year old body returned instantly. He felt healthy and strong and naked. On instinct, he quickly pulled a blanket over his lap as he sat on the floor of a large empty cave.

Luckily, he covered himself because six women entered the cave from behind a waterfall. William knew where he was. Somehow, he survived the fall from the cliff and the waterfall hid this cave.

He looked at the women again. They looked perfectly normal, except that they were miniature. Each had amazing, butterfly-like wings and each glowed with a different color, like the rainbow he believed saved him.

The one in the red dress approached him,

"Good to see you awake. I'm Ruby and these are my sisters. We are the Prismata."

"I've heard of you," said William, desperately wishing he had clothes.

Beryl, the green one, said, "I had to guess at your size, but I made you knew clothes."

And the blue one, Ultramarine, added, "I gave you some new armor. It's only a helmet, chest plate and shield, but I hope you like it."

William wrapped the blanket around himself and moved to look at the items spread out by the rocky wall. He saw a silky emerald shirt with brown pants and matching leather boots. The chest plate glistened and reflected the light emanating from the little women. The helmet had a tassel that looked like a short length of braided unicorn tail. He recognized the creature embossed on the shield. He picked it up and looked into the face of Evorin the dragon.

"This is amazing," William said. "I am already in your debt for saving me, these gifts are too much."

"We did not save you," said Ruby. "You saved yourself when you said yes, but I see you have already forgotten."

"Forgotten what?" asked William. It did seem like something important lingered at the edge of his thoughts, but nothing he could recapture. He knew he had a task before him and wanted to help Adam and Zandria complete their quest now.

The purple and orange fairies waited outside for William to dress and then offered him food. He felt strangely hungry, like he had not eaten in a long time. He wasted no time devouring a second and third serving.

As he finished eating, the yellow Prismata sat next to him. He looked down at her when she spoke.

"My name is Saffron," she said.

"The pleasure is mine," said William with his usual courtesy.

"I think there is something you are looking for."

William tried to think. It seemed she was right, but he could not remember what it might be.

He said, "Forgive me, but I am uncertain."

Saffron held up her tiny hand. In her palm, lie a single golden-brown seed. It looked no different than any other seed he had ever seen, of that he was certain. Still, he knew this one was special.

"Take this to the Queen of the Eastern Sky," Saffron said. "With it, only she can replant the Royal Forest. In time, the land will be whole again. You have done your part."

William took the seed from Saffron and immediately felt the warmth coming from inside it tingle throughout his body. He remembered Queen Olena was still at Castle Empyrean. That would be a long walk, he thought, but he stood up ready to start now.

"Rest, sweet William," came a voice from behind him. He did not know who he expected to see when he turned around, maybe his own mother. He turned to meet Ruby standing at his knees. She continued, "We have no intention of making you walk. You have had enough challenges for now."

The six sisters stood together in front of him. Their light started to shine so bright that all of their colors blended into white. Pure white light surrounded him until he could see nothing else and had to shut his eyes. William could not feel his feet touching the ground, but he did not feel like he was moving either.

When the light faded and he could open his eyes, William found himself standing in front of the huge wall of thorns that protected Castle Empyrean's entrance.

Down the hill, behind him, he saw two horses approaching. One carried a body draped across its saddle and the other carried two riders. Somehow, he had beaten Aleta here.

He greeted Sulis with a pat on his strong Friesian neck. Then Aleta jumped down and hugged him with her strong arms.

"I am relieved to see you alive, Prince," she said. "Though, I do not understand your presence here."

"Thank you. I am somewhat confused myself," said William, trying to catch his breath from her grip. "I must ask, why do you call me Prince?"

"I thought you were," Aleta said.

William stood thinking for a moment as the vines pulled back to allow them passage to the castle. Finally, he said, "Not that I recall."

Chapter 20

The Strange Creatures of Peckwood

Z andria cried.
  She cried for Dew.
  She cried for Eisenhahn.
  She cried for Professor Erbadin, Kalis and anyone else that stayed at the castle. She knew Shaydaway was evil, but she never thought he could go so far. They rode far away from the castle and could no longer hear the sounds of fighting. However, Tihi said things were not going well when she escaped.

  "Erbadin told me to find you," the horse explained. "I knew I had to get you and those crystals somewhere safe and Peckwood was the closest."

Adam said, "If Professor Erbadin is right about the power those crystals have, this is bigger than saving your mother now."

"Nothing is more important than that," said Zandria. "You don't know what it's like to lose your mother."

Adam jumped down from Tihi and the Friesian stopped. He looked hurt and mad. "You're right. I don't know what it's like to lose my mother because I never knew her. I was taken from her when I was a baby."

"I'm so sorry. I didn't think about what I was saying," said Zandria with that sudden realization. She climbed down too. Her heart quickly filled with sadness for both of them.

"It was a selfish thing to say," he added. Zandria knew he was right though. She had only been concerned for her mother and her own feelings since she found the first crystal. This was actually the first time she really even thought about Adam's parents.

He continued, "If that carnival man gets those crystals, we could lose more than your mother. We could lose all four queens, including your sister. I want you to save your mother. I really do. I want my mother back. But none of that will happen if those monsters get this Trammeler thing."

He dropped to his knees in tears. Beneath her anger and fear, Zandria could feel the warmth of Empyrean buried in her heart. That warmth brought a confidence with it that she wanted to share with Adam. She knelt beside him and started crying again as she hugged him.

She held onto so few memories of her mother from before Olena was born. She could not imagine having no memories at all.

"I never knew her," he said through heavy sobs. "I hope William can find her. I'm all alone here."

Zandria tried to comfort him, "You're not alone. You've got friends, like me." Her words were as much for him as for herself. She wanted to believe she could save her mother, but even with the energy given to her in the bell chamber, she still had doubt.

"It's not the same," Adam said. "When I was underground, there were all these kids. We were always working. I never thought about anything else. I risked a lot helping you and Olena. Now I'm helping you again. I never thought I would see my family, but because I'm here now, I don't even get that chance."

These words hurt. Zandria now felt like he was blaming her for what the dwarves did before she was even born. She knew he was mad and needed to work through feelings that he had not shared with anyone. She realized her old self would have quickly snapped back at him, taking the defensive. It made her feel better that she had this compassion for him. She wanted to share her feelings with him.

She said, "Adam, I promise we will find your mother. When we get out of here, we will see if William found her. If not, I will ask the queens to help. Even if they won't, I will help you. The two of us will find her together."

Getting his tears under control, Adam leaned back, still on the ground. He looked at her and she could see his mood changing. He said, "Thank you. It was my turn to be selfish, I guess. I needed to get that out because I really do feel better."

Zandria joined him, relaxing for a moment like they were on a picnic.

"When you helped me get into Castle Empyrean," Zandria said, "I learned a few things, about myself and this world. Sharing a burden makes it easier to carry. I know that might not make much sense. It wouldn't have to me a month ago. Remember, we're in this together."

Tihi neighed, waiting patiently.

Adam looked lost in thought for a moment. Then he said, "It makes sense. If I help you, then you can help me. I've waited this long and most of the time, I didn't even know what I was waiting for. There might not be anyone for William to find anyway. Besides, with the two of you, what more family do I need?"

"William doesn't seem like the type to fail," said Zandria. She truly believed what she said.

"If he doesn't turn into a baby first," added Adam.

"What are you talking about?"

"He started un-aging or de-aging or whatever you call it. He was still getting younger when I left him."

This shocked Zandria. "I thought he stopped getting younger when he reached his normal age."

Then Tihi neighed again. Zandria detected an urgency in this sound. She started to look around for what might have spooked the horse.

Adam whispered, "Don't move. We're being watched."

"Who could be watching..." she started to say.

Adam grabbed her head with one hand over her mouth to silence her. With the other hand, he turned her head upward, toward a tall tree. She scanned the branches and saw nothing. She shook her head, trying to let Adam know she did not see anyone. Then she saw movement among the broad green leaves.

Whoever it was must have realized he or she was being watched. The figure moved further up into the layers of branches. Zandria did not think one of Shaydaway's troupe members could have found them already. At least, she hoped not. Then she remembered Tihi telling her about the other inhabitants of the Northern Wood. She said something about the strange creatures of Peckwood.

Then, the spy completely disappeared. A small branch cracked and a leaf floated to the ground in front of them. This proved to Zandria that she did not imagine the figure.

"They know we're here now," Tihi said.

"Who?" asked Adam.

"Most likely the Skiordan," answered the horse.

"But is that good or bad?" asked Zandria.

"It could be worse. The inhabitants of Peckwood are not on the best terms with

Castlewood, but they are not outright enemies. It depends on who is watching us," said Tihi.

Zandria started to get worried. She said, "Are the Ski-whatever on good terms?"

"They've never hurt a human and seem to shy away from them for the most part. The Lochnobilians call them the Shadow People because they stay so well hidden," explained Tihi. "There are other creatures here that are definitely not fond of humans."

"It sounds like we should leave this forest," Adam said, climbing back on Tihi. He helped Zandria up on the front of the saddle and the Friesian started moving.

"Where could we go?" asked Zandria. "Shaydaway will be watching the North Road back to Castle Empyrean."

Tihi swished her tail. "Maybe we should try to make it to the West."

"That might work. There are more humans there," said Zandria. "What do you think, Adam?"

He did not answer.

Zandria turned around and Adam was not behind her. She did not know what made her look up, but she did in time to see Adam's feet vanish through the branches. She guessed it had to be the Skiordan that snatched him and pulled him up out of sight. Zandria thought maybe they were not as shy or friendly as Tihi believed.

Before Zandria could react, two pairs of hands burst through the leaves and gripped her. They lifted her up rapidly though the layers of the trees.

Below, she could hear Tihi whinnying and knew their captors were trying to lift her too.

Zandria could not see who was carrying her as tree limbs kept smacking her in the face. She wanted to believe it was not those acrobatic clowns. Still, she worried that the Skiordan might not be an improvement. What if it was some other creatures loyal to Shaydaway, she thought.

Then the fast climbing hands deposited her on a thick branch. She quickly checked that the pouch holding the crystals remained safe at her side. Adam straddled the branch below her. Below him, two creatures struggled to lift Tihi higher. Tihi did her own struggling. Eventually, the two attackers gave up and Tihi crashed back down through the canopy.

"Is she okay?" asked Zandria.

"I can't see down that far," said Adam. "I don't know."

The two creatures started climbing back towards them. They passed them and kept going straight up. Zandria got a good look. They were definitely not clowns, they must be the Skiordan Shadow People, she deduced.

She thought the Skiordan looked like grown men, but not quite. To start with, she saw these two had green skin. On their backs and forearms, they had patches of green fur. They both had long, fluffy tails. One tickled her when it brushed her arm as it moved up the tree. She did not know if the tail was stranger, or the fact that neither of them wore any kind of clothes. The only thing that scared her about them was the short curved claws on their hands and feet. She guessed these must help them climb.

Then they were alone.

Zandria saw that the branches grew so far apart and they sat so high up that there would be no safe way to climb down. She thought if she jumped from this height, she could end up with a broken bone or worse. She looked at Adam on the branch below and was afraid to even try to reach him.

"Now what?" asked Adam.

"I don't know. I hope Tihi's alright," said Zandria. "What do you think she will do now?"

Adam stood on his wide branch. As he talked, he stretched, fingertips grazing Zandria's branch. "She seems like a smart horse. She'll probably go for help. The question is, will she go back to Castlewood or try to go somewhere else?"

He could not quite reach her branch. He looked at their surroundings and began walking further out on his branch. He started doing a balancing act as the wood narrowed. Zandria worried that he might fall as he reached the spot where their branches mingled. The thinner wood out near the edge flexed under his weight. He used this to help him spring precariously up to her branch. Then he scooted in next to her.

"That's better," he said.

She felt better. She liked having him closer. It made her feel safer, too.

"These Skiordents," started Zandria.

"Skiordan," corrected Adam.

"Okay, Skiordan. They must want us up here for a reason. Maybe we should stay here until they come back," she said.

From far down below came a sound that chilled Zandria's heart. The unmistakable clink and clank of dangling pots and pans rang up to her. Shaydaway's cart rolled along on the very path they were lifted from only moments before. Zandria could not believe it. If the Skiordan did not bring them up into the trees, Raymond Shaydaway would have been right behind them.

The sound passed under them and kept going. Zandria knew they were hidden, but neither she nor Adam made a sound until long after the rattling faded. By the time either of them felt safe enough even to whisper, the sun had gone down.

"That answers your question whether they're friendly or not," said Adam. "I guess we're going to spend the night up here."

Zandria tried to get as comfortable as possible on their high branch. Adam insisted she sleep between him and the tree trunk to help keep her from accidentally falling in her sleep. Before Zandria drifted off, she looked above her. Through the few branches over her head, she could make out a beautiful, star-filled sky. She knew they were much closer to the top of the tree than the bottom. This thought made for needed, but precarious, sleep.

She awoke in the morning to a large pair of black eyes examining her closely. The eyes seemed to fill up most of the light green face of which they were a part. She found it strange that this

Skiordan's mouth would be above its eyes. Then she realized the face was not upside down, the entire body was. The creature dug its claws into the branch above her and hung down to look at her.

"Good morning," Zandria said timidly.

The creature bolted at the sound of her voice. It leapt, seemingly effortlessly, to another tree. Three other Skiordan, one each of pink, light blue and white, were sitting on several branches in that tree. They chittered to each other for a moment. Zandria thought they might scatter again. Then they became calm, almost eerily quiet. The Skiordan sat there, using both their hands and feet to grip the bark of the trees, so their backs and shoulders seemed permanently hunched.

Finally, Adam awoke. He seemed a little surprised at being watched, but not concerned by it.

"You guys got anything to eat?" he asked the waiting Shadow People.

The Skiordan chittered again. Zandria guessed they did not speak the same language as her, but they did not seem unintelligent. At least, she thought, they understood enough to know to help her and Adam last night. She wanted to tell them thank you, but the only way she could think to communicate it was to actually say, "Thank you."

The white one repeated back, "Daku."

This made Zandria smile. She said to Adam, "They can talk."

He said, "They're only repeating you."

"Daku," from the pink and blue Skiordan together.

Then a female Skiordan with soft looking yellow fur and yellow almost white skin appeared from somewhere below. Zandria noticed Adam blush when he saw she wore no clothes, like the males. Zandria did not feel embarrassed, Nookans were not overly fond of clothes either. However, she did become attached to the pretty dresses the last Queen of the Eastern Sky used to give her. There were plenty of villagers in Banookanook that went days without putting on clothes because they ended up getting too wet in the ocean or too hot under the sun. Still, she had never seen such colorful pastel people before, if she could consider them people and not animals.

The yellow female stopped on the branch below them. She reached up with an open palm full of fresh tree nuts.

"Breakfast," said Adam. He swiped the nuts from her and smashed them on the branch with the side of his fist. He picked through the cracked shells and offered Zandria the prizes he found inside.

Zandria could not resist saying it again, hoping for the same response. It felt like a game to her now. "Thank you."

"Daku," from the original green Skiordan.

Then the other three males chimed in, "Daku."

Lastly, the female said, "Daku?"

The green Skiordan chittered at the female and ended it with, "Daku." Then he sprang back over to Zandria's tree and landed upside down against the trunk. The claws on his hands and feet dug deep into the wood, keeping him securely mounted.

"Daku," said the female.

Zandria decided to call the first Skiordan Topsy because he spent so much time upside down. She thought Rouge would be a good name for the female. Obviously not because of her color, but because of what color she made Adam's face. Despite their recent troubles, their new friends put Zandria in a really good mood.

Topsy hopped down to the branch below them. He clicked his teeth at one of the other males and that one joined him on the thick branch. He gestured over his shoulder to Zandria and Adam. He clearly meant for them to get on the Skiordan's muscular backs. Zandria looked at Adam, still brushing shell crumbs from his hands. He shrugged and dropped down onto the Skiordan. Zandria cautiously followed his lead and lowered herself down to Topsy. She did not want to slip past and fall to the hard ground waiting below.

Without waiting to see if she had a tight grip, Topsy took off from the branch. The other Skiordan stayed right behind them. They leapt from branch to branch. Sometimes swinging from thin branches. Sometimes running on the thicker ones. They did not slow down even when heading straight for a wide trunk. Topsy would land on the trunk, grabbing it with both hands and feet. Then he would scurry around the other side and spring to the next tree. Once or twice, the jump would be farther than Zandria felt comfortable with, but none of the Skiordan fell or even stumbled.

When they finally stopped their frantic dash through the forest treetops, Zandria could not believe her eyes. Spread over the highest branches of at least fifty trees stood an amazing village full of every age Skiordan. Adorable, brightly colored children laughed and played while pale elders tended to meals. She instantly realized their colors must fade with age, as the oldest looking ones were mostly shades of whites and grays.

Zandria marveled at the Skiordan craftsmanship surrounding her. Ornate rails marked the edges of the multi-leveled decks. They must have carved every piece of wood by hand that made up the many small huts. The huts were grouped in circles of four or five, each circle surrounding a long, decorative table. She guessed that the different family members must live by each other and share their meals in one spot.

Topsy took them to the center of the village. There, the top of the tallest tree had intricate engravings all over its trunk. Zandria thought this might be their language, but it looked more like random designs to her. Rows of benches surrounded the tree, with enough seats for all of the Skiordan she could see across the village.

Zandria sat in the front row while Topsy went to gather the rest of the Skiordan.

Chapter 21

Tihi's Soliloquy

Friesians were not supposed to leave the ground, of that she was sure.

Tihi did not like being lifted up into the trees. The small hands with sharp claws surprised her as they grabbed her. Zandria and Adam disappearing only moments before shocked her enough. Now, whatever grabbed them held her. As she left the ground and started crashing through the branches, she bucked furiously. Because of her resistance, the creatures let her go. Then she started falling.

"That might have been a mistake," she said to herself.

Friesians were not supposed to fly, or fall.

She slammed the ground hard, luckily not breaking any of her legs. She looked up into the rustling branches hoping for a glimpse of Zandria or

Adam. Her sense of duty compelled her to try and rescue them.

Friesians were not supposed to climb trees, she reminded herself.

Tihi examined the branches, well out of reach even on her hind legs.

"Me, climbing a tree? Ha," she scoffed. She thought that would be about as likely as a Friesian climbing a mountain. No horse could do that. She looked around for any other possible rescue.

Nothing.

She hoped the kidnappers were Skiordan. At least then, she had a chance they might be friendly. While she had never seen Skiordan Shadow People, she had heard about them from some of the hunters back at the castle. Very few humans, dwarves or Friesians claimed to have seen them. The few reports were similar and usually ended with the Skiordan disappearing up into the trees. This encounter seemed to match the other experiences.

"I hope they're safe," she said. Inexplicably, she believed they were.

Tihi had a sense for these things. She also had a sense for approaching danger. Now, something triggered that sense to its maximum. On the path behind her, she heard the faint rattle of chains and the clink of swinging metal. The smell of the tortured donkey carried on the soft breeze confirmed to her nose who was coming.

"Shaydaway," she said. "I have to get out of here."

She felt leaving Zandria and Adam hidden high above would be the best way to protect them, as long as the Skiordan were actually trying to help. If Shaydaway caught her, he could torture her into telling him where they went, or worse. So, Tihi started galloping.

At first, she kept heading west on the path, planning to go to the Queendom of the Western Sun. Then she decided to challenge the deep woods and tangled undergrowth. She thought getting off the road long enough would allow for the wagon to pass her. Then she could double back to the North Road and race toward Castle Empyrean. After seeing what Shaydaway and his carnival did to Castlewood Castle, she could think of only one solution.

"Fury can help," she said to herself.

Finally, Tihi made it out of Peckwood and safely onto the North Road. Momentarily tempted to return to Castlewood, she stayed resolute and headed south.

She did not look forward to the great distance she had to travel across the plains. She knew it would take several days, even though she was already passing through Greatwood Forest. She did not want to think about the time it would take for the return trip with a rescue party.

Now, this was about her. She had to prove herself, not only to the Friesians, but also to herself. There was no stopping, no slowing, no doubting.

"I can make it," she told herself.

Then a triangle of bright light instantly opened in front of her and she disappeared completely into it before she could stop.

Chapter 22

Olena's Gift

Olena missed her sister.

Zandria had only been gone a few days, but Olena really did miss her. This was the first time in her life that they had ever been apart.

It excited her to be learning from the other queens and it distracted her. She had learned so much already in a short time, but the queens had hundreds, even thousands, of years of knowledge to share with her.

Mostly, this kept her mind off Zandria. Still, she wondered if her sister would find their mother. She really wanted her to. This also made her wonder if she would still be queen or if her mother would take over when she came back. Olena did not care if that happened because she would much rather have her mother than be queen.

As the days passed, Olena spent most of her time with Snow White, the Queen of the Northern

Wood. She had lessons about history. Cinderella, the Queen of the Western Sun, taught her about etiquette. On days that she spent with Isis, the Queen of the Southern Valley, they practiced magic.

Those were her favorite days and the days when she missed Zandria the least.

Isis told her, "There are some powers that we do not control. Sometimes, Empyrean must act through us, such as the day we repelled the Forgotten Evil."

Olena tried to comprehend what Isis told her, but some things were difficult to understand for her six-year-old mind. She felt like she had grown up a little since becoming queen. Still, some days she felt too young for the things they were teaching her.

This became a topic that Kez and Sylvan discussed with much interest.

In what little free time she had, Olena enjoyed the company of her dear friends.

The wise quzzak Kez would swing from the bedpost by his soft, fuzzy tail. He seemed to be adapting quite easily to life in the crystal castle. This surprised Olena since he had spent his entire life in the wide-open jungle.

She worried that her two friends would feel cooped up being restricted mostly to her bedroom because of the magically transforming hallways.

At least, she thought, the room seemed bigger to the toy-like Sylvan. His little wooden body stood no taller than her hand from fingertip to wrist. More for her own pleasure than necessity, Olena painted a crude face on his smooth, round head. Her young hands were not as steady as she would have liked, so

Sylvan's smile appeared slightly wobbly and one eye was definitely larger than the other.

Today, they discussed the strange conversation she had with Zandria right before her sister left.

"Queen Isis did say sometimes Empyrean could act through you," reminded Kez. He let go with his tail and sailed from the bedpost into a waiting pillow. This seemed to be a rather childish activity in which the old quzzak repeatedly indulged.

"But it felt more like I was watching from outside," explained Olena. "I don't even remember what I told her."

Sylvan's high, squeaky voice bounced off the glass walls, "In my many years of service, I have found more often that it is better not to question things I do not understand."

"He's right," Kez added, "in a way. The other queens would not allow you any harm inside this place. Besides, you always have us."

One morning, Isis wanted Olena to try something new. For this, they stood side by side in the open courtyard. Tym, the elven butler, watched from the stairs and even Fury came from the stable to observe.

"Do not worry if you cannot do this," said the fierce queen. "No queen has been able to create a Walking Portal for a thousand years."

"Why should I try then?" asked Olena. She doubted herself enough because she was a little kid. She did not want to fail when she tried something new.

"The portal is a gift. Either you have it or you do not," said Isis. "Not since the Passing Queen has anyone had it."

Olena wanted to ask who the Passing Queen was, but Isis interrupted her thought.

"Put your hands like this," she said, sticking her arms out in front of her. Olena copied her, opening her palms away from her body. Then Isis touched her thumbs together and slowly turned her hands inward until the fingers of both hands made a triangle.

Nothing happened.

Olena followed the same motions. When her fingers touched, a bright light formed in the space between her hands. It started to move away from her and grow larger, keeping its shape. Surprised, Olena quickly let go and the light faded. She turned to Isis, afraid of being reprimanded for stopping.

The Queen of the Southern Valley looked stunned. She hugged Olena and then turned to Tym.

"Elf," she said, "tell the other queens she has the gift."

Tym dashed into Castle Empyrean without a word. Isis waited by the door.

While they waited for Snow White and Cinderella to come outside, Fury came to Olena's side.

He reassured her, "I knew you could do it."

"But I don't know what I did," said Olena, truly not knowing. Isis remained out of earshot, waiting by the door.

"My queen once told me about the portal," Fury said. "She wished they all could do it, because it is a way to instantly walk anywhere in Empyrean. You see how that would be quite helpful in times of great danger."

When the three queens finally approached her together, Fury respectfully moved back by the stable. The sight of the three old ladies giddily moving as quickly as they could toward her made Olena laugh. They looked ancient, but acted like young girls, she thought.

"She can do it without saying the words?" asked Cinderella, finishing a conversation they must have started without her.

Isis nodded and then excitedly said to Olena, "Please, do it again."

Olena nervously raised her hands. She did not know if she could do it again because she did not know how she did it the first time. She stretched out her hands and touched her thumbs together like before. Almost before her fingers completed the triangle, the bright light appeared. This time, she did not let go and the triangle grew larger as it moved away from her. In a moment, it was tall and wide enough that she guessed even Fury could pass through it with a rider on his back.

Then, as Olena imagined, a Friesian did barrel through directly at her. At the last second, Isis used her own magic to push Olena out of the way. Otherwise, this new horse would have trampled her. Isis' magic lifted Olena and gently sat her down out of danger. When she landed, she let her hands down and the triangle disappeared.

Olena squeaked out a surprised, "Ka."

Fury must have recognized the horse and said, "Tihi? What are you doing here?"

Tihi's diamond shoes skidded across the glass floor near the steps. She stopped and quickly looked at her new surroundings.

"I was in the Northern Woods," she said, looking stunned by her sudden change in location.

"You can talk?" said Fury. Olena did not understand why that would puzzle Fury.

Snow White stepped up to the Friesian mare. "Don't act so surprised," she said. To Tihi, she said, "Tell us what happened."

"I knew I had to get to Castle Empyrean," said Tihi, trying to catch her breath. "One moment I was escaping from the Northern Wood and the next I was here."

Isis said, "You can thank the new queen for that. She has the gift of the Walking Portal."

Olena joined the conversation. "If she came through, doesn't that mean she was in some kind of danger?"

"You learn quickly," Snow White said, putting a hand on Olena's curly head. "Please tell us what is the matter, Tihi."

The horse briefly recounted the tale of searching for the crystal and encountering the Carnivale Chaotica.

"Professor Erbadin sent me while he and the mighty Eisenhahn remained to defend Castlewood Castle. I went to aid Zandria and her young friend when they escaped the siege. I lost them in Peckwood Forest. Please forgive me," she concluded.

The Friesian lowered her head.

"It is no failure of yours," said Snow White. "I know nothing of this Raymond Shaydaway, but he seems quite powerful. You did more than can be expected."

Aeran, the captain of the guardian hawks, spiraled down from above, "Your majesties, travelers are approaching."

Snow White turned her attention to the front gate. After a moment's concentration, she whispered the spell to open the protective briar. Olena tried to concentrate too. She knew the castle could tell her who was coming near, but she had not mastered that technique yet. Nor had they told her how to call back the thorns. The other queens had no intention of allowing her out until they were sure it was safe and she was ready.

When Tym completely opened the front gate, Olena saw William approaching with a few of the others that had gone to rescue the slave children. He looked as young and strong as she imagined he would have on the day he froze five hundred years ago. They crossed the temporary bridge and Olena saw Snow White shed a single tear at the sight of the unknown soldier's body. Whoever he was, Olena thought, the northern queen must have known him well.

Now it was William's turn to tell his tale. Olena did not like his story any better than Tihi's. It had too many sad parts and she felt bad for Fury losing so many Friesians. Then William knelt in front of her.

"A friend of yours asked me to give this to you," William gently placed the Prismata's golden seed in her hand and she immediately felt it's magic. Then he finished by explaining Adam's parting with Kalis and how he finally tracked down Lord Vanril after they lost Terg. He kept the news of being Adam's uncle to himself. He still wanted to tell Adam first of his discovery.

Then it was agreed that Olena should open the Walking Portal once again. This time, William and Aleta would go to the Northern Wood to rescue Zandria and Adam. The queens decided that the two of them might be more effective and definitely faster than an entire army. Olena did not know how long she could hold open the Walking Portal, so the small size of the party relieved her.

"William, you can have my saddle," offered Fury.

"Begging your pardon," said Sulis. "I've grown quite fond of the lad."

Fury looked a little dismayed, but agreed that William should ride Sulis. Olena suspected the man and horse formed a strong bond in their recent travels.

Aleta bowed, "It would be my privilege to have your saddle, General Fury."

At that, William and Aleta mounted Sulis and Fury. Olena opened the Walking Portal and without further preparation, they left.

She hoped they would make it in time.

Chapter 23

A Ticket to the Carnivale Chaotica

Zandria grew nervous as the many colorful, fuzzy faces started to surround her. They took turns examining her, some gently poking, some sniffing too closely. Topsy, the first green Skiordan she met, dashed around gathering the others. They filled the benches of the meeting area quickly, but not before each completely inspected her and Adam.

While these furry people with their long tails and sharp claws looked strange to her, she tried to imagine how she looked to them. She had no tail and only the hair on her head. Her skin was tanned from normal sunlight. A lifetime of sunny days on the beach turned her skin a healthy tan, but her color was not nearly as impressive as the children inspecting her apparently inadequate fingernails. She guessed their chittering to be wondering how she could climb anything with her tiny claws.

She looked to Adam and saw him acting extremely uncomfortable. The clotheless creatures pressed in around him as well. He apparently did not like being so much the center of attention. Relief spread across his face when the yellow-tailed Rouge shooed the others away. Then she sat next to him and his face turned redder than any of the Skiordan babies.

Finally, Topsy stood in the center of the group near the decorated tree. He whispered in their clicking language to an elderly gray male with a thick black stripe down his back and tail, who sat in a separate and obviously special chair. Zandria clearly heard Topsy say "Daku" and the elder looked puzzled.

"Daku," said the gray elder to Zandria in a cracked, but friendly sounding voice. She smiled, not knowing how to respond. Then all of the Skiordan said "Daku" like a chorus.

Adam laughed at this. "Be careful, Zan. They might make you their new leader."

She did not think this quite as funny as Adam did, but the thought did amuse her. She could not help but imagine herself sitting on her own beautifully carved throne. The Skiordan would bring her nuts and berries while she taught them her language.

A sudden shift in the wind pulled her from her reverie. Topsy and the other Skiordan did not look panicked and Zandria even thought the breeze felt familiar. Then a cyclone swirled in front of them and Bajuk, the forest guardian, spun out of it, landing on his tiptoes next to the gray elder.

The wood spirit-in-training did not appear in his rabbit costume like the last time Zandria saw him. This time, he wore a short white robe with a gold coronet in his grass-like hair. She thought the miniature crown made him look more like royalty than a wood spirit. She assumed he must appear differently to the different peoples of the Northern Wood. Still, apparently, he could not change the shape of his short, round body with even shorter arms and legs.

Bajuk briefly greeted Topsy and the elder Skiordan before coming over to Zandria. He bowed to her and said, "So we meet again."

"Are you a spirit yet?" she asked.

"Alas, not yet. However, your situation may help my cause along," he responded. "I have some news of your elven friend and her captors."

Zandria jumped up with concern, "Is Dew alright? Where is she?"

"Easy, child," said Bajuk. He gestured with his stubby arms for her to calm down. "By reuniting the two of you, I may save these woods from a great tragedy, thus earning my honorable place."

"What about helping others?" said Adam.

She knew he was right. In her heart, she knew it was more important to do right and good for the sake of others than for one's own benefit. Still, if Bajuk wanted to help them for his own gain, then she would take advantage of that to save her friend.

Bajuk looked offended by Adam's words. He said, "I do what is best for the forests of which I am responsible. Wood spirits are beyond the quarrels of humans. However, I do not like to see anyone suffer either."

The short protector turned back to Topsy. They had a brief discussion, unintelligible to Zandria, which led to Topsy chittering with the elder and the elder addressing all of the Skiordan.

Finally, Bajuk spoke again to Zandria, "The spirits have found the campsite of that carnival man. The Skiordan here are not warriors, but have agreed to take you to them. That is all I can do."

With that, he twirled up into another cyclone and disappeared. After a few moments, Topsy, Rouge and a group of brave adult Skiordan gathered around Zandria and Adam. The rest of the families returned to their normal daily life around the village. Topsy signaled for Zandria to get on his back.

"I guess they're ready to go," said Adam. Zandria could not wait any longer and quickly pulled herself up on Topsy's back.

Rouge offered to carry Adam, but he shyfully opted to ride with a tall powder-blue male. Then the rescue party leapt into the branches. This time Zandria enjoyed the ride, knowing what to expect. The jumping and swinging made her laugh despite the coming danger. She wished she could move like the Shadow People did without the fear of falling. The Skiordan were fast and did not hesitate at risky jumps. Soon, they were in the western part of Peckwood Forest.

The rescue party spread out across a few trees and Topsy pointed below them. Through the thick leaves, Zandria saw the frighteningly familiar sight of Raymond Shaydaway's wagon parked at the end of a small clearing with the donkey still hitched to the front. The interlopers that survived the fight at Castlewood Castle busied themselves setting up some of the smaller tents. She saw a few of the tents finished and recognized one as the unfortunate unicorn's prison.

Then two of the sinister clowns emerged from the tall cart, carrying Dew by both arms. Zandria shivered at the thought of their creepy hands on her. They dragged the elf across the small clearing toward the unicorn tent. Dew struggled fiercely all the way. The clowns pulled her inside the tent and came out a moment later without her.

Zandria whispered to Adam, "Did you see that?"

"Yeah," he said. "Did you see that?"

She followed his pointing finger to Shaydaway's wagon. On the back corner hung a wire cage that she did not remember seeing before. Inside, nested the golden seagull Crumb. She saw no sign of Professor Erbadin or Eisenhahn and hoped they were safe. Zandria worried now if anyone else even survived the attack on the castle.

As if Adam read her thoughts, he said, "Don't worry. I don't see their strongman, so Eisenhahn must have beaten him. That cowardly ringleader probably ran from the castle the same time as we escaped. I'm sure Eisenhahn and the others are fine."

"How can you know that?" she asked, wanting to believe him.

"Think about it. Tihi must have run back to Castlewood and now they're all coming to save us. Maybe we should wait until they get here."

Zandria did think about it. She thought, if Adam was right, there is no way Professor Erbadin, Kalis or any other Friesian could find them. She did not even know where they were. The Skiordan took them all over Peckwood and Shaydaway did not seem likely to stop where he would not be safe either.

"We can't wait," she decided. "I can't leave Dew down there. She wouldn't leave me." She had only known the elf a short while, but she knew this was true.

She started to climb down, but Topsy grabbed her arm. He gestured for her to get on his back. Then he climbed down much quicker and quieter than she could have. He lowered her to the ground directly behind the unicorn tent and out of sight. The blue Skiordan deposited Adam right behind her. Then the creatures vanished back up into the higher branches.

Adam lifted up the edge of the canvas and they crawled inside. They came up silently behind Dew. The clowns tied both of her hands roughly to the center post. The unicorn noticed them first and gave a weak neigh. Zandria tried to comfort the tortured animal and gently patted its bruised side.

As soon as Dew saw her, she said, "What are you doing here? Get out of here."

"We're rescuing you," said Adam, already cutting the ropes with his short sword.

"Don't you know this is a trap," said Dew. "He's expecting you to try to save me."

Remembering her promise, Zandria busied herself unbolting the shackles around the unicorn's ankles. She looked over her shoulder at her friend and said, "He doesn't even know where we are. We have some help."

"Don't be too sure. Shaydaway has power over these animals. You can't trust anybody, especially Peckwood creatures," said Dew.

"I trust the Skiordan," said Zandria, briefly glancing upward.

Adam finished cutting Dew's ropes. She rubbed her free wrists. "The fuzzy tree-climbers? At least they're loyal to the Queen," she said.

Zandria loosed the last of the unicorn's shackles.

Before Adam could say, "Don't let her go", the unicorn stampeded away. In a panic, Zandria and Dew scrambled for the back before anyone could be alerted by the freed unicorn.

An instant later, the curtain rustled and Raymond Shaydaway ushered himself into the tent.

He said, "Going so soon? The show's about to begin."

Two clowns ripped open the back of the tent and several interlopers followed behind Shaydaway. Adam had no choice but to surrender his sword. The henchmen led them out into the center of the close circle of tents. The magician Lazarou stood waiting next to a short figure. Zandria could not believe her eyes when she realized it was Bajuk.

"You betrayed us," she shouted.

The wood protector answered, "I did what was best for my woods. Mr. Shaydaway promised to leave the Northern Wood once he had you and the Trammeler. I could not risk the safety of those under my protection."

Dew said, "You can't trust him. If he gets the Trammeler, even your great spirits will be his slaves."

The wind came up as Bajuk prepared to leave without debating it further.

Shaydaway gestured to Lazarou and the magician waved a hand that froze Bajuk in place. Suddenly, Zandria could not move either. She looked to her right and saw Dew and Adam struggling in place, too. She thought, Lazarou's magic must be strong.

"No one's leaving now," said Shaydaway. He circled behind Zandria, Dew and Adam, his long thin legs stepping deliberately. "Mr. Lazarou, if you please, on with the show."

Lazarou smiled, or at least it appeared to be a smile on his cracked, lipless face. The whites of his eyes seemed to shine in the black oval of his face. He snapped his fingers with both hands and they burst into flames. He shot fireballs randomly into the trees, seemingly unaware of the watching Skiordan.

Zandria saw Bajuk's face turn to a look of horror as he realized his mistake. She guessed Bajuk led them to Shaydaway after he made the deal that he thought would rid the woods of two problems. Now his plan to become a wood spirit was going completely wrong. Instead of saving his forest, he caused it damage.

Then Shaydaway stepped up in front of them. He bent low over Zandria. With an exaggerated gesture of putting the back of his hand next to his mouth, he whispered, "My magician friend likes to play with fire. I wonder how your friends fare with it?"

"You can't do this," snapped Zandria.

"I can do this," he said. "You see, I serve the Forgotten Evil. It is my honor and duty to do this. Once I have captured the queens, then my Master can return. And this is my encore performance where I once again request the crystals. Spoiler alert, this time, I get them." Raymond Shaydaway paused for dramatic effect. Then he said, "But that should not be a surprise ending to you."

"No, but this should," said a familiar and friendly voice.

Zandria looked around to see William charging atop a Friesian that looked almost identical to Adam's friend Kalis. Fury followed close behind, carrying a strong southern woman.

They were being led by Tihi and, in front of her, the escaped unicorn.

Shaydaway dived out of the way of the galloping horses. Lazarou lost his concentration and his magic spell broke, letting Zandria and the others free.

Bajuk began shouting up into the trees, "Daku, daku."

Topsy and the other Skiordan must have understood his call and dropped from the branches. Clowns and interlopers were suddenly being lifted into the air never to be seen again. The Carnivale Chaotica had become quite chaotic.

Zandria tried to escape into the woods, but a clown jumped to block her path. She turned around to see Lazarou coming toward her, forming a new fireball in his hands. As Lazarou prepared to throw the fireball at her, a gust of wind extinguished the flame. Bajuk's cyclone swirled past and the little man snagged Zandria clear of the danger. Lazarou did not look like he expected the flame to return. As soon as Bajuk's wind died down, it instantly engulfed his entire body. The magician issued a long, silent scream and exploded into fiery ashes.

On the other side of the clearing, Zandria saw Saman the deformed dwarf watching the fight from atop the wagon. When William rode near, the dwarf jumped down onto his back. In one swift move, William flipped the evil dwarf onto the ground and finished him with a deft slash of his sword.

"I've had enough of dwarves for a while," he said, heading toward his next attacker.

Bajuk let Zandria down next to Adam and then bounced clear of the fray. She helped Adam open the cage holding Crumb. The bird immediately flew up to safety. Dew ran up next to them.

She pointed and said, "Look."

Zandria looked. William and the warrior woman were fighting the last two scary, acrobatic clowns. It seemed that the Skiordan helped defeat the interlopers. The fight was almost over.

Then Zandria saw Shaydaway standing in the middle of the clearing. His tall hat smashed and his white suit covered in dirt, he looked uncontrollably furious.

"You've ruined me," he spat when he talked. "I lost those crystals six years ago, but not before I tested them. I know their power will work on the queens or even someone going to be queen. I could rule all of Empyrean with them. I could even have been more powerful than my Master."

Zandria now knew this man imprisoned her mother. She hated him for it, but she wanted to ask him how they worked. How could she free her mother?

Before she could respond to him, a broken, golden horn appeared in the center of his chest. Zandria did not understand what happened until she realized the tortured unicorn speared him from behind. The wicked carnival man fell limp and slid off the horn to the ground. The unicorn ran off into the woods, finally free.

As soon as Shaydaway fell, the remaining interlopers vanished. Zandria hoped they returned to their own worlds, but somehow doubted Shaydaway would release them even in death. Then she felt a relief that she had not felt in a long time. Being finished with Shaydaway made her glad, but she feared she might need him to learn how to use the crystals.

Now, that did not matter. Adam, William and Dew stood with her. The Skiordan helped them and even Bajuk redeemed himself. Zandria looked at the little man with the grassy beard and thought she could see right through him.

"Bajuk, what's happening to you?" she asked.

He tried to look at himself as he grew fainter.

"I did it," he said. He looked surprised.

Then a strong breeze blew through the clearing and he disappeared. This time, he actually became the wind instead of only riding on it. The breeze circled them once. It rushed past them ruffling their hair and clothes and then it was gone. Bajuk earned his place as a true wood spirit and that made Zandria happy.

William mounted the Friesian he called Sulis. Then he offered a hand to Adam and the girls climbed up on Tihi. Aleta and Fury waited ahead of them. Crumb circled above and headed east.

Zandria said to Topsy, "I'm going home now. Thank you for all of your help."

Hanging upside down from a low branch, the Skiordan blinked his big black eyes and said, "Daku."

Chapter 24

Four Into One

The trip back to Castlewood Castle passed thankfully uneventfully. Being reunited with her friends and having the four crystals elated Zandria. Also, she felt a great relief that Shaydaway would no longer be chasing them.

She felt even safer because Topsy and some other Skiordan decided to escort them to the edge of Peckwood Forest. They scrambled among the branches above her, occasionally skittering to the ground to grab a fallen nut. Then they slipped back up into the leafy covering. Crossing into Castlewood Forest, she could hear them calling after her, "Daku. Daku."

Zandria sat behind Dew and Tihi carried them between Sulis and Fury. The southerner called Aleta remained quiet, but Zandria immediately liked her. She seemed strong in both body and spirit. With a strong personality like hers, Zandria thought she could become fast friends with the independent elf that sat in the front of Tihi's saddle.

Zandria also noticed how William snuck glances at the dark-skinned warrior. On the few times their eyes met, William and Aleta would exchange smiles. Zandria suspected something had changed in William since she had seen him last. He seemed revived, but she did not think meeting a new woman could do that to a man. Maybe she was wrong, though.

While she thought about William, she listened to his conversation with Adam. He recounted the journey from the Palace by the Sea to Bond and then to Soria Moria.

When he started to speak about finding Adam's birth records, he said, "I'll come back to that." This seemed to annoy Adam, but he also appeared to want to know what happened with Vanril.

William concluded with the defeat of Lord Vanril and the seed he received from the Prismata. Zandria wished she could have been there to see those colorful fairies again. Finally, he told of his meeting at Castle Empyrean.

"I think you will be most interested in this," he said, turning to Zandria. "It seems your sister has been gifted with one of the queens' ancient powers. She can open a Walking Portal and instantly travel anywhere she wishes."

This excited Zandria. She was so happy for her sister becoming Queen of the Eastern Sky. Now, it made her happier to know she had special gifts as well. She asked William, "They didn't even have this power in your time?"

"What time would that be?" he said with a cross between a smile and a look of confusion.

"You know, the olden days."

"I would have to look in a history book for that," he laughed.

This seemed odd to Zandria. She wondered why he acted like he forgot being frozen for five hundred years. When she looked at the others, they looked back at her like she did not know what she was talking about. Something told her to forget about it, so she said nothing else.

William spoke again, "Now, there is one other piece of news I have to tell you, Adam."

Adam twisted around backwards to halfway face William. Zandria believed he must be bursting for any news of his mother or the rest of his family. Adam did tell her that William promised to search for them after he returned the children to Bond.

"There is no delicate way to put this," William ran a hand through Adam's copper hair and then held the boy's head. "I found documents stating that your parents are no longer with us, but..."

Adam started crying. Zandria wanted to cry for him too.

"But," William said, fighting back his own tears. "But, I did discover that I am your uncle."

Adam cried harder. He wrapped his arms around William in a tight hug that almost knocked them both from Sulis' back.

Strangely, the news did not completely surprise Zandria. She expected that as much as they looked and acted alike that there must be some connection. Then she thought maybe it was the power of the queens that gave her this extra insight. She seemed to be the only one aware of William's past and the likelihood that he and Adam were related. Maybe it was the heart of Empyrean still burning in her heart that helped her know this, she imagined.

Finally, they were in sight of Castlewood Castle. Apparently, Tihi, Fury and Sulis could not wait any longer and galloped straight for the broken castle doors. There, signs of the recent battle littered the courtyard and scarred the walls and no one had started repairs yet.

Zandria saw the giant Eisenhahn crouching next to the door like an enormous metal boulder. When Eisenhahn saw them, he stood up, grinning.

"Horsey, you brought my Adam back," the iron man said to Tihi.

Then Eisenhahn reached up and hugged Adam and William both in one embrace. After that, he moved to Tihi and hugged the girls in the same way. He tried to hug Aleta, but she offered a handshake instead. They moved into the courtyard where Professor Erbadin and his dwarves came to greet them with Kalis and some other Friesians.

"You may rest here for as long as you need," said Erbadin. "However, I have been informed to send you to Castle Empyrean as soon as you are ready."

They dined together and slept in comfortable beds in front of cool Peckwood fires that night. In the morning, Zandria felt ready to go back to the four queens. She desperately wanted to solve the mystery of the Trammeler and knew that would not happen here.

Professor Erbadin prepared a fine coach with a harness for four horses. Fury, Kalis and Sulis moved into position without being asked. Tihi stepped up to the fourth spot.

She said to Erbadin, "I would like to be on the team if I may."

The dwarf looked at her with a puzzled expression.

"She can talk," said Fury. "Surprised, huh?"

"No," said Professor Erbadin. "I knew she would have something to say when she was ready. Her mother did the same thing. I'm impressed by her sense of duty, though. Of course you can go."

The stablehand harnessed Tihi and the others while Zandria and her friends boarded the carriage. Despite Eisenhahn taking up two seats, they were quite comfortable. Adam almost sat next to William, but Zandria guided him to the seat by Eisenhahn. Then the only seat left for Aleta was next to William. Zandria took the spot next to Dew and the two of them giggled at the older couple now holding hands.

The trip to Castle Empyrean passed leisurely and could not be over soon enough for Zandria. Finally, one afternoon, they were passing through the enchanted briar that guarded the main gate. The horses pulled them across the temporary bridge and then Zandria heard the click of their diamond shoes on the stone courtyard. The sight of the towering crystal spire filled Zandria's heart with peace.

Tym the elf waited at the top of the steps that led into the castle. Zandria watched the team of magnificent Friesians as they were escorted to the stable. Then she followed the others inside.

As Tym navigated the changing halls to the queens' throne room, he talked with Dew.

"So, how is the clan?" he asked.

"Still treating me like I'm a child," she said.

"Better get used to that. The old lady called my mother elfling until she left home at the age of one hundred and twenty."

Everyone laughed at that, including Dew.

Then Tym added, "I would be willing to vouch for you here, of course."

Dew looked thoughtful for a moment. She said, "I'm not sure that's in my blood. Besides, someone has to keep Zandria out of trouble. Maybe I'll see what she gets into next."

After that, they arrived at the throne room. The queens sat waiting on their thrones, except Olena. She raced to Zandria and hugged her. Zandria loved the welcome and did not realize how much she missed her sister.

"I helped you as best as I could, Zan," said Olena.

"I know. Thank you," replied Zandria.

"Oh," Olena turned to William. "I waited for you."

She grabbed William's hand and led him to the high balcony facing east. Zandria watched Olena take a large seed from some hidden pocket in her beautiful robe. She showed it to William and then threw it out the window.

Instead of dropping down with the meek throw of Olena's tiny arm, the seed shot up into the air. It flew due east out of sight. Then in the distance, a bright flash, like a single star, lit in the sunny sky. Zandria guessed it was far enough away to be over the Dead Forest and maybe over the wasteland.

"I can't wait for you to see it," said Olena, starring off into the East.

"You have my thanks, your majesty. I think I should ask your leave in the morning to return home. Adam would you care to join me?" said William.

"I want to wait with Zandria to see if we can help her mother."

"I would love to see your homeland," volunteered Aleta.

William looked a little surprised, but mostly pleased. He said, "It would be my honor."

William and Aleta stood together near the doorway.

Adam started to appear agitated, "Give them the crystals, Zan."

"Thank you," she said to Adam and then presented the four crystals to the four queens.

"This is called the Trammeler and my mother is a prisoner inside it."

Snow White stood, "We will do everything we can to save her, but for that, you must leave us now."

The next two days felt like the longest in Zandria's life. None of the queens, not even Olena, left their throne room. Zandria heard that they did not stop for meals either. Adam and Dew kept her company during this time. They tried to distract her with other activities, but she could only think about her mother.

The worst part for her was that she had no dreams each night. Her mother did not come to her at all to give her any hints or words of assurance as she had during her quest.

On the third morning, Dew woke Zandria up by knocking sharply on her door.

"I found out some interesting news last night," said the unusually cheerful elf.

Zandria tried to rub the sleep out of her eyes. She had no idea what Dew meant.

"Tym introduced me to the Empyrical Wizards," continued Dew. "They're kind of stuffy, but they can read the stars better than my grandmother. We found out a fact about today. Can you guess?"

Zandria did not feel like guessing. She hoped someone was delivering news of her mother. Instead, it appeared that Dew wanted to play a game.

Zandria said, "I give up. Is it Queen's Day?"

"No. It's your birthday," said Dew with a giant grin.

It took a moment for Zandria to realize what the elf said. It felt like a long time since anything normal happened to her. Celebrating a birthday seemed strange to her now. She had to concentrate to remember how old she would be.

"That means I'm eleven now," she reminded herself.

"Right. And Adam and I made you a cake."

That morning, they had cake for breakfast. It was the biggest cake she had ever seen. Only a few times before, at the market in Edge Town had she even tasted cake. To her, this was the most wonderful of all. Having her two best friends make it for her made it all the more special, despite being lopsided with multiple colors of icing smeared over it.

Eventually, Eisenhahn joined them. Apparently, he had never tasted cake. He laughed loudly with each bite.

Zandria washed down the gooey mouthfuls with a big glass of milk. In one particularly long gulp, she opened her eyes to the bottom of her glass. She almost dropped the glass because she thought she saw someone staring back at her. The figure turned and she saw it was her mother.

Then she heard a voice that sounded far away, "Four into one, Zandria."

The image of her mother faded into a strange crystal shape. It seemed to be a pattern made by joining the four separate crystals.

This time, Zandria did drop the glass. It broke on the floor, but that did not bother her because she was already running out of the room, shouting for Tym. Adam and Dew chased her, but Eisenhahn stayed behind stuffing his mouth with cake from their leftover plates.

"I know what to do," she shouted back at them.

Before they were lost in the castle's changing maze, Tym caught them.

"I heard you calling, my lady," he said.

Zandria was out of breath, "Please take me to my sister. I know what to do with the crystals."

Tym did not hesitate. He rushed them along and in a few minutes, they were standing outside the door to the throne room.

Olena swung the door open before Zandria could knock, "I wondered how long it was going to take you."

"I know what to do," said Zandria again. She did not stop to ponder what Olena meant. They must have been waiting for her to have this vision.

"I expect so, because our magic isn't working on it," explained Olena.

Each of the queens presented one of the crystals to Zandria without questions. Zandria took them to the center of the room. She lay on the floor on her stomach like she was building a toy puzzle.

Zandria leaned the first crystal on its end. Then she leaned the second crystal against that, making a triangle shape with the floor. When she let go to get the third, the first two collapsed.

She looked to Adam for help. He must have understood her wordless plea because he quickly joined her.

Now, Zandria started over. She positioned the first crystal and Adam held it in place. Then she positioned the second crystal. As she reached for the third, Dew knelt down to hold the second one in place. Finally, Zandria leaned the third crystal against the others to make a pyramid. She carefully let go and the others followed her lead.

The three-crystal pyramid stood on its own. Zandria stood up and held the fourth crystal upright over the top of the pyramid. She let it go, hoping it would not knock over the other crystals or smash on the glass floor.

It did neither.

The crystal simply hung in midair where she let go of it above the pyramid. Then a beam of blue light shot up from the three crystals below to the hanging fourth. The floating crystal gently slid down inside the light until its tip touched the top of the other three. When they touched, the blue beam fanned open into a wide archway.

A woman stepped out, looking unsure of where she found herself.

"Mother," shouted Zandria. She ran to her and her mother welcomed her with a hug.

In that moment, nothing else existed for Zandria. She dreamed of this for so long, now that it was real, it still felt like a dream. She had no words to describe the need she had for her mother's arms. It was a perfect feeling that she thought was gone, never to be replaced. In this embrace, she was completely safe. There was nothing but love and security here. It was a feeling that she knew could not come from anything else, even the deep magic of Empyrean.

Zandria tried to squeeze six stolen years into that hug, but her mother had to let go. She knew her mother had to hold Olena, because she never had the chance before.

Olena came over, timidly. When she felt the woman's arms around her, she closed her eyes and started to cry, "Oh, mommy."

While Zandria watched through her own tears, she heard whispers behind her that she was probably not supposed to hear.

Cinderella said, "What does this mean for the Queen of the Eastern Sky? Will the Lost Queen take her place?"

"I do not know," whispered Snow White.

Zandria wanted to turn around and say something, anything. She discovered that she could not turn because both of her friends were holding her hands, one on each side. She saw that they were crying for her too.

Then the woman let go of Olena and stood to her tall, elegant height. Olena stepped back and Zandria wrapped her arms around her sister.

"Zandria, thank you for setting me free," said her mother.

Zandria knew what was going to happen next. She said, "No, it's too soon."

A warm light started to emanate from within her mother. Zandria could see specks of gold dust begin to rise out of her hair and off her simple white dress.

"I love you both."

"We love you too," said Zandria through her tears.

Then the woman's entire body began to disintegrate into the golden dust, rising and dancing into the air. Almost as quickly as she appeared, she passed over into the twilight.

Zandria feared this would happen because a new queen is only called when the old queen is gone. She wanted more time with her mother. She wanted to tell her about Olena and their father. She wanted things to be like they used to be. She wanted desperately to have her mother back.

Still, Zandria felt nothing but joy to have finally set her free.

Olena did not know how to feel about meeting her mother and losing her on the same day. She did not have the memories her sister had.

Still, knowing the woman was finally free gave her a sense of peace. Zandria seemed to be dealing with it fairly well on her own.

One thing Olena did not know was that she would never be allowed to tell her sister what happened to the Trammeler.

Her duty as a queen required her to witness the four crystals sealed in a small wooden chest. Each of the shards had its own place embedded in a specially shaped cushion.

The Empyrical Wizards carried the case to the bell chamber at the bottom of the castle. Olena and the other queens watched as they dropped the case into the misty depths of the bottomless canyon.

As the case faded out of sight, Olena hoped those crystals would never harm anyone again.

Before she left the bell chamber, she wondered what else those wizards might have dropped into the white mist over the years. She did not know if she would ever ask for an answer.

Chapter 25

Ten Years Later

As Olena had promised at the Feast of the Rockhorn Battle, Soria Moria was fully restored and given to Zandria as her home.

In the short time that the Palace by the Sea eroded back into the beach, Soria Moria grew to exceed its original magnificence. Due to the many deeds that Zandria did in service of her sister, the Queen of the Eastern Sky, every artisan and craftsman across Empyrean leant his skill to the restoration.

The tower stood tall and proud. In front of the castle, a western gardener named Humboldt planted a beautiful garden surrounded by the lush greenness of the Royal Forest. A new road connected Soria Moria directly to Bremen. That town had once again become the way station for traveling east to the Queen's new home, the Palace on the Sea, floating off the coast of Banookanook.

Like Soria Moria, Zandria changed as well over the last ten years. Gone were the days of awkwardness. Her body was now that of a beautiful woman. She and Olena both looked so much like their mother, but both exceeded their mother's beauty. Zandria carried herself with grace, yet she had the strength and poise she gained throughout her travels. She was courted by many for her looks, but more widely known for her caring nature and generous heart.

However, there was only one man in her life now. As Zandria grew into womanhood, her friendship with Adam grew into romance. Nothing came between them with the challenges they faced. On their many adventures, they formed an unbreakable bond.

Lately, Zandria spent many days in the Great Hall. There, she would lounge on her favorite couch, staring up at the ceiling. Its glass had all been replaced and every track set in motion. As the enormous kaleidoscope slowly rotated, the Great Hall danced with unimaginable color. The stained glass far above her head was especially important because it now depicted the past adventures of her and her friends.

Today was different for her, though. Today, Zandria celebrated her twenty-first birthday. She planned to celebrate it with a wedding.

Her elven friend Dew Lantisphere, not looking much older than the day they met, rushed around behind cooks and florists checking the preparations. Her sister, Queen Olena, helped her with an exquisite dress. Olena's advisors, Kez the quzzak and

Sylvan the wooden doll, had many helpful comments. The other queens arrived and Apis the black cat roamed the halls of Soria Moria.

In the Great Hall, a highly polished Eisenhahn greeted guests and ushered them to their seats with his usual childlike enthusiasm. The guests included dwarves like Professor Erbadin, elves, Nookans, Skiordan, Bondsfolk and many other friends Zandria made over the years.

Outside, Crumb the gold seagull circled with Guardian Hawks and other Bremen birds. Admiral Mildoo Vol fired canons from his ship in salute. An old warhorse named Wrath and his unicorn mate Sayonya watched over their offspring, black unicorn colts, with the Friesian General Fury. The dragon Evorin roosted on the highest parapets and gave a mighty roar.

With everyone seated, Ruby, the eldest of the Prismata sisters, started the ceremony. William escorted the stunning bride down the aisle to a waiting copper-haired man. Adam smiled when he saw Zandria in her gown. Then William joined his wife Aleta, seated in the front row.

As Ruby recited the ancient words of marriage, Zandria could only think of one day that rivaled her feelings now. She thought for a moment of the day she rescued her mother from her crystal prison. She wished her mother and father could be here. Then she felt that old, familiar warmth in her heart and she knew they were.

A tear trickled down her cheek as she said, "I do."

About this book

Can you miss someone you never knew?

Zandria and Olena's mother has been missing for the past six years. In many ways, it's like they never knew her at all. The pain of their loss is realized the night after the great battle. Zandria discovers a hidden crystal imprisoning their missing mother.

This discovery sends Zandria on a new quest, while Adam leads a rescue mission of his own. However, the wicked ringleader of the Carnivale Chaotica, Raymond Shaydaway, has plans of his own. He is intent on stopping Zandria and bringing back the Forgotten Evil.

Will Zandria escape the evil Carnivale Chaotica? Will she find her mother in time to save Empyrean again?

The Search for the Lost Queen begins!

About the author

As a best-selling author and publisher, Mark has won various awards for writing and book cover design.

Growing up in Kansas, Mark graduated from Sumner Academy of the Arts and Sciences and received his Bachelor's in Film from the University of Kansas.

Mark has written under a few pen names with numerous novels, screenplays, short stories and digital series to his credit.